# DARK TALES – VOLUME 1

I0551889

## Edited by Dorothy Davies

# DARK TALES – VOLUME 1

GRAVESTONE PRESS

# TABLE OF CONTENTS

# Night In Our Veins (Paul Edwards)

"What are you doing?"

Ethan looked up, and I managed to catch a glimpse of the picture he was drawing in his sketchbook – some demonic-looking creature with large, scabrous wings and the blackest of eyes.

"It's what's been calling me," he said. "The only thing that makes sense."

"What is it?"

"Don't know," he replied, shrugging. "But it wants me. And the emptier and more lost I am the better." He turned back to his work, picking up a piece of charcoal from off the table.

I left him to his art, feeling uneasy and concerned.

Ethan and I ventured out that night for the first time in a long time, finding a quiet corner in an otherwise bustling *The Raven Inn*. I thought going to the pub might do us both some good, but he was as distant and morose as ever.

I tried engaging him in conversation. "I rang my brother up earlier."

He sneered but said nothing.

"He thinks I should contact my parents. Maybe they've changed. What do you think?"

He put his bottle of Diamond White down on the table, then wagged his finger at me. "Your parents are selfish, self-satisfied people. They want you to embrace everything they value." He reached out, touching me lightly on the arm. "You should have grown up like them, didn't you know? Career-minded. Conservative. Deathly dull and completely uninspiring."

"Alex says they want to mend things. They want to know me again."

He shot to his feet, knocking into the table, clearly exasperated. "I'm getting another bottle. Do you want one?"

I shook my head and he wheeled away, jostling his way to the bar.

Later, as we stepped out into the night, I told him, "Sorry."

Ethan's shoulders sagged and he looked heavenwards.

"It's just that… I've been thinking a lot about my family lately, you know?"

"Why?" he said. "After what they put you through, you should just fucking forget them. Forget they ever existed."

"It's not as easy as that…"

"They don't mean anything to you anymore, right? You've moved on. What's the point in looking back?"

I stared down at the pavement, thinking: *Why can I never find the right words in an emotional conflict?*

"Hey," he said, softening his voice, touching my shoulder. "I want to take you somewhere."

He led me to a church on the outskirts of Cosham. It was run-down and boarded up, its walls smeared with graffiti. The silence and stillness of the place felt dislocating, and I shivered beneath my jacket. "Why are we here?"

Ethan didn't reply. He reached into his coat pocket and pulled out a bottle of Diamond White.

"Smuggled this out of the pub," he grinned, peering around me at the church. "By the way, you heard the legend about this place?"

I shook my head.

"Something moved in there and made itself at home. Hiding inside the church or in the graveyard somewhere, I'm not sure which." For some reason I thought of that strange creature he'd drawn in his sketchbook the other day.

He turned his gaze on me, his smile gone. "If you can prove you're serious, if you can show *it* what it wants, then it'll gladly take you in."

He necked his cider, then squeezed and cracked the bottle in his fist. Broken glass fell, sprinkling the earth. He held his hand up, inspecting the wound. "Don't bleed anymore," he whispered. "It's like the night's running through my veins."

"Come on," I said, taking hold of his arm. "Let's get out of here."

\*\*\*

I woke the next morning to find Ethan gone; I was all alone in his bed. I forced myself up, shuffling out of the room and into the hall. His boots and coat were missing and a glance at the clock revealed I was due at work in under an hour. I dressed and was soon driving my rust-eaten Metro through town. I stayed away from the main road, choosing to pass the church we visited last night instead. It was there that I saw him, traipsing through the graveyard on his own.

*You heard the legend about this place?*

I stamped on the brake, pulling up on the outskirts of a housing estate. It didn't take long to find a payphone – there was one outside of a convenience store near the King Richard School. I told my boss I was suffering from a migraine, but I don't think he believed me. *Fuck him,* I thought, slamming down the phone.

To the west there was a hill overlooking the church. I walked to the top of it, watching Ethan use his shoulder to break through the church's double doors below.

I closed my eyes, listening to the branches of the trees clack around me. My mind backtracked; I reminisced over the first couple of months of our relationship, and how I'd thought – *I've never known anyone quite like Ethan.*

He was unique, beautiful, scary. He always wore black T-shirts, a long leather coat and a pair of scuffed Dr. Martens. To look at, he reminded me of that actor Vincent Gallo, from the movie *Buffalo '66*; pale, gaunt face, unkempt hair, intense grey eyes embedded in cavernous sockets. He said from the outset that he didn't believe in love, that he'd never had that feeling for anyone and probably never will. That wounded me at first, and perhaps a stupid part of me hoped to turn him around. Now I know better.

He let me move into his flat shortly after the fall out with my parents. Occasionally we'd go out drinking, but mostly we stayed in, ensconced within the flat's walls. Ethan would sit on the windowsill, staring through the glass with such intensity that I'd swear he was projecting images from his mind onto the dismal wastelands below.

He introduced me to poetry, reading aloud from the works of Plath, Poe and Larkin. We'd stay up into the early hours, reciting our favourite poems or listening to indie-rock on his beaten stereo. Sometimes Ethan would draw with charcoal, producing weird and disturbing images in his sketchbook. I think his winged demon disturbed me most, though. In time Ethan grew disinterested in art; he withdrew into himself – away from the world, and from me, too.

I remember the first time he caught me alone with my straight razor.

"We really do belong together," he said, an enigmatic smile flickering across his face.

I opened my eyes, blinking, refocusing on the world around me.

Ethan had finished his exploration of the church and was now pulling closed the gates. I thought about going down there and joining him, but I didn't really feel like it; I felt strangely hollow and detached from things.

I returned to my car and waited until he was out of sight, then drove up to Portsdown Hill. I parked in a secluded spot overlooking a grey sprawl of tired-looking tower blocks and houses. The sea on the horizon was clean and white, like a thin strip of mercury.

I opened the glove compartment and took out the plastic case inside. It might have been a snap-case for a pen, toothbrush or comb. I unclipped it and tipped out my straight razor.

I tilted the seat back and rolled up the sleeve of my shirt. I put the razor to my flesh and began cutting, Ethan's voice echoing around inside my head: *"If you can prove you're serious, if you can show it what it wants, then it'll gladly take you in..."*

I gasped, the blade slipping through my fingers, clattering onto the pedals by my feet. I lifted my arm up, staring in disbelief at what I discerned beneath the flesh...

\*\*\*

The flat was silent, chilled. I threw my jacket onto the sofa and stood staring out of the window. The sky was grey and lightless and I prayed for rain to come and break the monotony. It reminded me that I hadn't cried in such a long time. Suddenly I heard a noise coming from the bathroom. I turned around, calling: "Ethan?"

I found him in the bathtub, his eyes fixed on nothing in particular on the wall. For a horrible moment I feared the worst. Then he blinked, the grin spreading across his face looking like the rictus of something long dead. "Found it," he breathed.

I turned away, prompting him to sit up in the bath and ask: "When you're ready, you'll come, right?"

"Yes," I said with my back to him. "You know I will."

I heard his razor scrape across the rim of the bathtub. I looked over my shoulder, watching him cut himself.

"I'm ready," he whispered. "Just waiting on you now. I never wanted to do this alone, remember?"

*It's a comfort to the damned to have companions in misery,* I thought, and wondered where I'd heard that from. A line from one of the poems we used to read, I supposed.

Something surfaced in his eyes then; something almost human, I sensed. He suppressed it, blinked it away.

"Cut me," I said.

He sneered as I offered him my arm. Then he stood up and slashed me.

Seconds later the razor dropped into the tub with a splash. "You too," he said, so faintly I wasn't sure I'd really heard the words.

He cupped his long, cold hands around my face and kissed me hard on the mouth, but I tasted absolutely nothing of him at all.

\*\*\*

I followed him through the streets, past lines of shuttered shops and crooked townhouses. The moon looked like a rip in a sheet of black fabric. *Just another hole,* I thought, absently.

We reached our destination, clambered over the padlocked gates and dropped down into the grounds. Bone-white headstones and marble angels hovered in the darkness around us.

Ethan took hold of my elbow, guiding me toward the church doors. The pale moonlight fell in a spectral slat over that splintered entryway. Ethan pushed on through, produced a small torch from his pocket and flicked it on. Everything seemed buried beneath layers of dust and cobweb. His light paused momentarily at a wooden pew that had been pushed aside, and I saw the raised lid of a trapdoor.

We shuffled forward, Ethan crouching and pointing the beam down into the blackness. "There's a ladder set in the wall," he said. "Watch yourself." He carefully mounted the rungs. "Coming?"

I turned my body around and lowered my boot onto the first rung, then slowly followed him down. I reached the bottom, brushed the dust off my jeans and turned. He used the beam to show me that we were in a chamber as small and sparse as a tomb.

I gasped when I saw the statue; it looked so lifelike, so *real*.

Ethan's face twitched; a spasm that wasn't quite a smile. He put the torch in my hand so I could point the beam at it myself.

It looked like it was carved from onyx, its arms folded, its long-fingered hands gripping its bony shoulders. Scabrous wings protruded from its body.

It stood on a cracked plinth and, as I raised the beam, I swear I saw it smile.

I placed my hand to my chest, to my pounding heart, then took it away again. Thoughts of my family passed through my mind.

*They want to mend things. Want to know me again.*

I glanced nervously at Ethan. "What is it?"

"We have to show it." He stared at me, emotionless. "That we've passed the initiation. That we're ready and willing to submit."

He produced his straight razor from his pocket. Rolled up a sleeve and rested the blade against his arm. He pressed down, the flesh opening blackly.

*I don't bleed anymore.*

I glanced around again at the statue.

Its smile was clearer now, wider. Directed right at us.

I was shaking all over. *Mustn't let on I'm afraid*, I thought.

"Your go."

Ethan raised the gleaming blade in his hand and I rolled up the sleeve of my shirt. He cut me quickly, keenly, causing me to shut my eyes and close down and focus on detaching myself. I opened my eyes at last. The wound was deep. Blood was trickling down the inside of my arm.

I sensed movement and jerked the beam, seeing the statue step down from off its plinth. I tried to scream but no sound would come out. It shuffled forward, hooves clopping, wings unfurling, cupping its clawed hands around Ethan's face. Then I wheeled, bolting through darkness, groping for the rungs of the ladder and scrambling up them.

Near to the top I paused, twisted around and directed the beam into that sepulchral vault. I screamed at last for I could see the thing had wrapped Ethan up in its wings, its clawed hands still cupping his face, its mouth fastened to his throat. Ethan was shrivelling away beneath me, the creature sucking in all that terrible nothingness. Then the thing let go and lifted its face, casting its abyssal eyes on me.

*It'll gladly take you into itself...*

I scrambled up the rest of the rungs and emerged into the nave, tossing away the torch, crawling along on all fours toward the church doors. I dragged myself through them, found my feet at last and took flight, screaming, shrieking all that emptiness out of me.

The next thing I knew I was out of the graveyard, staggering around in circles under haloes of hazy streetlight. On the fringes of a housing estate I found a callbox by a lonely 24-hour kiosk. I closed myself in, leaned back into the darkness and sucked in long, steadying breaths of air.

I rummaged through my pockets for loose change. Grabbed hold of the phone receiver and punched in a number I somehow still remembered.

A familiar voice answered.

"Mum?" I said, my own voice shaking. "Mum, it's me, Violet. Sorry it's late." I swallowed a sob, wiping the tears from my face with the back of my hand. "Mum... I want to come home."

# The Quiet Ones (Liam A. Spinage)

"Five more last night." Arlette's voice was tired, scratchy. Jacques looked up from his patient in concern, not just for Arlette's voice but for the voices of so many others.

"That brings us to twenty-two." Jacques' broad shoulders slumped momentarily. He'd been up for thirty hours straight and knew he had to get some rest. He also knew that rest wouldn't come. Not until he had an answer.

"How can twenty-two people suddenly lose their voice?" Arlette's query was spattered with a light raspy cough and muted by the handkerchief she held over her mouth as she spoke. "What do you think, Doctor?"

"I don't know. It's possible there's a natural explanation. I'm not entirely convinced until I do some more tests."

Arlette narrowed her brow and turned her head away slightly. She'd been working with Jacques at the Hope Springs Mission for a couple of months now and thought she had the feel of the man. He rarely spoke and even when he did, there was much he didn't say. She'd come to understand that what he didn't say was just as important as what he did. If he wasn't convinced there was a natural explanation for a sudden outbreak of what might well be laryngitis, then that meant he thought something else was at work. Namely, a supernatural element. That made it her territory, not his.

"I'll ask around. See what people know. At least, the part that they're willing to say."

Jacques nodded wearily. At this rate there wouldn't be anyone left who could say anything, willingly or otherwise. There were few enough people in this forsaken place as it was. Most of those were troubled and traumatized. Perhaps that's what had drawn him here in the first place. He had wanted to be a doctor from a young age, No, scratch that, what he had really wanted to be was a healer. There was a subtle difference in those words. He wanted to make people better, make the world a better place. It seemed fitting that the world had responded by putting him in a place where people really needed him. He stifled a yawn and walked over to the sink to wash his hands.

*\*\*

Arlette stepped outside the mission and looked down the street. At one end was the edge of town, where the road petered out into abandoned fields full of rotting corn stretched across the valley floor. She had thought about treading that road many times. Of getting out, like so many did. Somehow she never managed to take that first step. There always seemed to be something drawing her back in. Behind the mission were the remains of what she once understood to be the lake, the crater caked now in a red-brown sludge of mud and rust. Even the spring, which had given the mission its name, had dried up. It was as if even fresh water - hell, anything fresh, wanted nothing to do with the

18

eternal seeping entropy and decay which inculcated itself into every sinew, every fiber of one's being if one had been here long enough.

Arlette had been there three years.

In the other direction lay the mass of squalid shanties which separated them from what she liked to call the heart of darkness - the largely abandoned town center where the buildings were tall enough to cast long shadows over the rest of the town and where people rarely ventured these days. Everything salvageable or stealable had been taken years ago. There was little left to loot. Arlette set off toward those shanties, past the boarded-up gas station and across alleys strewn with broken glass and equally broken lives. She knew who she'd approach first to try and get an answer. She only hoped she'd get there in time.

***

When he'd first rolled up here, the name of the mission caused Jacques to break out in a rare wry smile. There were no springs here anymore where the mountain had once given up its waters in torrents to feed the lake below. He knew enough geology to understand where those falls must once have been, how majestic they must once have looked. Once he'd gone inside the dilapidated building and found it empty, he also understood there wasn't much hope, either.

What there was, still, was a mission. Not capitalized as it was on the creaking sign which hung half-heartedly outside the place, but the mission he'd felt a calling to all his life. He'd tried to leave his own demons behind when he'd left Canada, but they had followed him incessantly, hounding his every move. Very well, he decided. Time to pick a battleground and meet them head on. Within days, he'd managed to salvage a few essential medical supplies. One day later, he had his first patient. Three days after that, that patient had become a conspirator against the darkness in his own life, just as he had in hers. When Arlette had first walked into the mission, her arms had been crisscrossed with bloody scratches so much that he'd feared a serious infection. Even then, she'd refused to say what had caused them. She hadn't needed to. As their eyes met in a flash of understanding, he knew they were somehow self-inflicted. He'd eventually teased an answer out of her, but that answer had come with additional questions. Fearful dreams, dark thoughts. Long screams in the night borne of a pain she carried inside which she felt compelled to make manifest on her body as she struggled against what she'd found here.

"Here be monsters." She had pointed toward the town as they sat outside the mission. "And here," she admitted, pointing to her head. "And here," pointing to his. Jacques merely nodded and they'd watch the sun go down and darkness fall, hand in hand, then arm in arm.

A lot had happened since then. Jacques didn't really understand what Arlette meant about the darkness in the heart of town. He'd assumed she

20

was talking metaphorically. Now, he was sure she wasn't.

He had two patients with severe burns and no more painkillers. And twenty-two patients with what looked like laryngitis but wasn't. There was no cough, no splutter. What he could see when they tried to speak wasn't the exhaustion of someone with an illness, it was the exasperation of someone who can't express anything but fear, confusion and anger.

Jacques had had some success with calming them down, getting them to write what they needed on paper. There were a few problems here, though. It seemed that the neighbourhood hadn't attracted a literate crowd. Hardly surprising. Many of his patients struggled to read and write at the best of times, but when they were in this state, they found it even more difficult to articulate. To top it all, the paper got moldy quickly. Ink dried up at an alarming rate. Pencil leads broke almost every time they were used. It was frustrating.

Currently he was encountering that frustration first-hand in the person of Davey Winters who didn't need a larynx or a pen to tell Jacques just what he thought of him. Not when he had two huge fists to do the talking for him.

\*\*\*

Arlette, meanwhile, had stopped to catch her breath at a dime store a few blocks over. Here, Sara was busy setting out the stalls outside and swatting off the bluebottles that had begun to buzz around

21

angrily. She did this every morning with a blend of defiance and precision which Arlette found comforting. Sara was the only person Arlette knew who'd been here longer than her, which she thought made her the longest-standing resident of Prosperity. Sometimes, Arlette wondered what kept her here. Deep down though, she knew the answer. Like so many others, Sara simply had nowhere else to go.

She looked over at the display of goods Sara had available. The usual array of scavenged parts, the few unlabelled tins of presumably-food. Arlette had bought one of those tins once and it had turned out to be rice pudding. She wasn't a fan, but had eaten it anyway, straight from the tin with a little spoon she kept in a makeshift pocket - little more than a tear in the lining of her fleece.

"Hi Sara. How's things?"

Sara smiled and waved Arlette closer. She was normally more talkative than this. Unless…

Damn it all. You were my last chance.

Sara pointed at her throat and shrugged as Arlette swore quietly under her breath.

"You wanna come down to the mission and let Jacques have a look at it?"

Sara shook her head, her dreadlocks whipping animatedly as she did.

"Ain't no point," she seemed to say. After a protracted series of points and gestures, Arlette understood. "We both know that what's doing this ain't something he can fix."

"You got any ideas?" Sara saw and heard a lot as she scavenged her way through the city. Things

22

that might be crucial to understanding how to deal with this. Or at least understand where it was coming from.

Sara shook her head again, then appeared to change her mind. She beckoned Arlette inside the shop. Arlette followed, knowing if nothing else there would be good coffee.

\*\*\*

Jacques managed to dodge the first blow but succumbed to the next two. Say what you like about Davey, but he still had a good right hook. Both their faces were contorted now, Davey's with rage and Jacques' with pain. Fumbling in a pocket, Jacques staggered backwards, fumbling in a pocket, managed to steady himself momentarily on the edge of a nearby cot before the flurry of Davey's blows became almost too much to bear. One punch sent him reeling across the floor, arms raised over his face in defense, giving him a few precious moments to get the syringe from his pocket. Now all he had to do was get in close enough to use it without causing any further harm to either of them. Davey loomed over him, red-faced and panting. Jacques thought he saw his chance and reached up, grabbing hold of the thin cotton of Davey's bloodstained shirt and dragging him down on top of him. When he went to administer the sedative, though, Davey countered with a jarring headbutt which knocked it out of his hand. The pair of them rolled around on the floor for what seemed like an age, neither of them landing any blows, just trying to disentangle themselves from each other. Davey grabbed him in a choke hold, threatening to draw out the last of Jacques' breath just as his own had been cruelly stolen from him. He was about to pass out when he felt Davey suddenly go limp on top of him, drool forming at the corner of his mouth. He rolled the unconscious Davey off him and there stood a smiling Arlette, syringe in hand. His savior.

"Sara's lost her voice too."

They'd managed to pick up Davey between them and deposit his body unceremoniously on a makeshift bed. He'd recover soon enough, but they'd have some time to deal with the root cause. Jacques just hoped that time would be enough.

"I can't imagine Sara ever being quiet." Jacques winced as Arlette applied a cloth to his head wound.

"I know what you mean. Still, she showed me something on the map. She's seen something over at the old civic center. Here, look, she gave us an artist's impression." Arlette unfolded a sheet of paper and showed it to Jacques. It looked like the after-impression of a Rorschach test, all blotchy interlocking circles in shades of gray. Jacques wasn't sure whether to be impressed at the artist's hand he didn't know Sara had or to recoil in abject horror that this arrangement of muted, faded shapes might be something which had a physical presence in the town he'd come to call home.

Arlette watched him chew this over in his mind as she passed him a dented Styrofoam cup of coffee she'd brought back from the shop for her.

24

"Here, soldier, reckon you'll need this."

"Thanks." Jacques downed it on one, desperate to be more alert if not more refreshed. He winced.

"It's not that bad!" Arlette's gentle jibe woke him more than the coffee had.

"It's awful!"

"I guess you just get used to it. It's the best we got."

They both paused.

"You're going over, aren't you?"

Another pause, longer this time.

"We. We're going over. I'm not doing this alone; I'll need you there with me. Whatever it is, we'll deal with it. Besides, do you want to be here when Davey comes round?"

Jacques groaned.

"Thought not. We'd best get a move on if we're going to get there and back before dark."

It seemed he had little choice in the matter.

***

"Why do you do it?"

They'd reached the three-storey civic hall and paused while looking for the best way inside. The main doors stood impressively intact in their off-white marble with Greek columns on either side, laced with little cracks that had taken their toll over the years but still standing tall. Above them, a clock hung over the main entrance. It had long been abandoned by its hands and numbers. Just another faceless entity in the town, a reminder of what grandeur had lived here once.

"Why do I do what?" Jacques knew what Arlette meant. They'd had this conversation before, many times.

"Help people." Arlette spat in the road; her phlegm thick with the strong, black, awful coffee.

"You know why. They need it."

"OK, so why don't you help yourself while you're at it? Physician, heal thyself, right?"

"I can't. At least, not like that.

Arlette decided to change tack.

"Need to heal everyone else first, right? Like you're the Fisher King?"

"Well, this is certainly the Wasteland." Jacques managed a laugh, then retorted. "Why do you do it?"

"Why do I do what?" Arlette was enjoying the circular conversation.

"Keep looking. Investigating. What do you hope to find?"

"What makes you so sure there's something there to find? Ready to believe in the supernatural finally, man of science?"

"Spare me your jabs of mockery!" Jacques laughed again, but his face became serious. "I'm ready, I think. This place..." He didn't need to say any more. As if in response, what sun managed to permeate the low hanging mist had firmly retreated behind a looming array of murky gray clouds.

"Right on cue." That's what Arlette intended to say, but it came out differently. What she actually said was "......"

Jacques looked up, wide awake now. "Arlette?"

26

Arlette was frantically trying to indicate something to him, but he wasn't sure what. He thought - out of the corner of his eye - that he saw the tiniest shadow escape from the corner of her mouth and zigzag its way to the marble doors, only to get lost in the rest of the shadows. Surely a trick of the light? No, he said to himself. He had to be ready to believe.

First, though, he had another patient to deal with.

\*\*\*

Arlette had collapsed to the ground in one of her frequent coughing fits but managed to recover quickly enough and shot him a scathing look which he interpreted as "Are you ready now?" She produced two flashlights from her fleece and handed one to him. He rolled it over in his hand and tested it by twisting the end. It flickered briefly but shone well enough. Arlette had done the same.

They both nodded to each other and climbed the stairs to the marble doors. They didn't need words to understand each other's intentions. Not anymore.

\*\*\*

It took their combined strength to lever the door open just a fraction, but that was enough to let them in. They looked around, flashlights gleaming paths. In the mist-choked darkness, these little paths of light showed long-forgotten pews, signs and documents. Whatever order might once have held sway here, it had long departed and left in its wake a ramble of rubble, all discarded bureaucracy of former lives. Human beings were not meant to enter these doors, not anymore. No sun or moon entered here. Nothing did any more. The central hall was silent as the grave but so much worse. The grave, after all, holds either the promise of finality or the chance of another life, a better life, an afterlife. There was no such hope here.

Arlette threw a pebble at Jacques to attract his attention. He was shivering in the sudden cold, standing there open-mouthed.

Snap out of it

Jacques tried to speak. Tried to articulate what it was he was looking at. To put it into words. All that came to mind was all the voices from his past which had wounded him. His abusive father. Angry patients. An angrier girlfriend. They all told him the same. He was never going to amount to anything. He was useless. He was wrong. He was a waste of space.

All the voices said that, except one. Somewhere, somehow, amidst the sound and fury, one voice rang clear. It was Arlette's.

"Believe!"

And he did. Not just in the amorphous, slowly circling shapes which seemed to be edging forward towards him. Not just in the supernatural and otherworldly explanations which his rational mind had always wanted to dismiss.

For the first time in ages. Jacques believed in himself.

It was an absolute rush. He screamed out loud, all the repressed fury and rage and guilt within him came out in one long breath as he reached up to wipe the tears from his eyes.

The form stopped moving.

He screamed again - louder than before - and Arlette's voice joined him, camaraderie in cacophony. Hundreds of voices then flitted between them, every soul silenced now released in a bitter, primal scream with only one message to convey. "Enough," it said. Not as a plea, but as a rallying cry. "Enough."

The monstrous form shifted in the shadows, turned and gave flight. Jacques fell to the floor, exhausted, and Arlene collapsed again, gasping with new-found breath. It would appear that for the time being that they had won out.

The darkness would come again, as it always did. But neither Jacques nor Arlette were willing to go gentle into that good night. Not while there was still hope, or while there was still a mission.

# Culprits (Olivia Arieti)

Somebody was roaming in the attic, Debbie was sure of that, but whenever she went up, silence and darkness were the only presences. Lately, dreadful nightmares kept troubling her night and day; too much pressure, too many things had happened in that horrible year. She broke up with Barry just a few weeks before the wedding and shortly afterwards, the guy died in a terrible accident. Nobody had been able to explain how on a sunny morning his car, out of control, crashed into a tree, but all agreed that the poor fellow was deeply depressed and harshly condemned her behaviour, especially when rumours of her new affair spread. As a matter of fact she had fallen for Ryan, a dubious, but charming fellow who easily won the hearts of all the girls he set his eyes on. His long term hatred and rivalry with Barry fuelled his desire and he swore he would take Debbie away from him no matter what.

One evening, when her fiancé was on a business trip, he knocked at the door.

"Simply wanted to say farewell to the loveliest bride-to-be in town," and added, "Are you sure you want to do it?"

Debbie looked at him surprised, but without giving the time to reply, Ryan took her in his arms and kissed her so passionately that she wished he would go on forever.

"Have you gone mad?" she mumbled.

"Yes, baby, mad for you," and kissed her even more wantonly.

Then he suddenly let her go and walked out.

Even if not married yet, Debbie felt adulterous.

The fire had been kindled and lust was all over and under her skin. She tried to reason, meditate, understand, but the emotions were too strong, the passion too intense. Now Ryan only was in her thoughts; his burning touch had marked her heart.

Other encounters followed and when Barry arrived with the rings, she called the wedding off.

Both disconcert and discomfort showed in his eyes now fixed on hers.

"Who is he, Debbie?"

The girl lowered her glance; she couldn't hurt him that much.

"Killing you would be foolish," he shouted in an unfamiliar menacing tone, "but not the asshole who did this to me."

It didn't take him long to find out who his fiancée's lover was.

"I'll get her back, you bloody cheater, she'll never be yours," Barry shouted to his rival.

His words disturbed Ryan; although he considered the guy incapable of extreme deeds, he was well aware of his deep love for the girl. An unnerving uneasiness got hold of him and wicked thoughts followed. He would never let her go, even if it meant plummeting straight to hell.

What was only a threat soon turned into a plan; a few nights afterwards, Barry followed the treacherous bloke home.

The sinister glow of the brand new knife appeased him, but as he got nearer his prey, he began shivering, already disgusted by the bitter scent of blood. His hand was trembling and his heart pounding so loudly that he let the weapon fall.

Sweat mingled with tears as he cursed his stupid weakness. He wasn't a murderer and never could be.

A few days later, the deadly accident occurred.

Although Debbie felt responsible for her late fiancé's dejection and feelings of guilt overwhelmed her, she couldn't have wedded whom she no longer loved.

Now Ryan was the one about to move in with her once the knot had been tied.

The house was old and isolated, the exterior decayed and the interior, despite the new furniture, maintained its grim aspect. The attic with gables and a cellar damper than a castle's dungeon provided, apparently, the perfect lodgement for uncanny presences.

On hearing again moans and thuds, Debbie went up; dust and cobwebs tapestried the trunks, boxes and the antique chest of drawers.

"You shouldn't have done that to me," a hollow voice cried, "My heart is still bleeding," and desperate sobs followed.

Barry's spectre was right before her.

"You have doomed me to everlasting grief, Debbie."

"I've simply been fair... to both of us, besides, the accident wasn't my fault."

Shudders pervaded her on realising she was talking to a spirit.

"I won't abandon you, I'll be your guilt forever, my dear, you deserve nothing else."

That said, he vanished in the darkness, leaving her as dismayed as distressed.

Once back in her room, she burst into tears. Her sobbing went on for long for the spirit's words had literally stabbed her heart. Surely, now it was bleeding too.

She kept tossing and turning all night; guilt was worse than regret and remorse devoured her soul. Probably her rightful punishment.

When a week later Ryan arrived, eager to set the wedding date, Debbie showed no enthusiasm.

"Let's wait a little more, honey, Barry passed away just a few months ago and I might be considered vain and... heartless..."

She, too, was condemning herself.

His insistence vexed her. Why so anxious? Recently, his glance had become furtive, his expression, tense.

"No, I won't wait any longer," he cried like a stubborn child on the point of stamping his foot. No excitement or desire filtered from his voice, only annoyance and impatience.

Then his face darkened, "Can't risk Barry coming back and making you change your mind."

Debbie gazed at him perplexed. What scared him so?

Now she was looking forward to the ghost's visit, convinced that her new fiancé was hiding something, something horrid, perhaps...

"I was about to kill the lurid bastard," the spectre confessed one night, "but hadn't had the courage."

He added, "I've sinned all the same, though... My love for you has dammed me."

Then he silenced, lowered his eyes and if grief, wrath and despair ever had an image it stood right before her.

Never had she felt more miserable.

"Whatever, my death wasn't accidental, the brakes weren't working."

'Impossible,' she thought, 'the car was new... He bought it to drive her around the country during the honeymoon.'

A terrible suspicion struck her... One person only could have wanted him dead...

The following day, the hope of a revelation drove her to Barry's tombstone.

Nothing stirred, nothing moved, the wind had forsaken the cemetery and all spirits seemed fast asleep in their graves.

The thought of being the cause of the two men's hideous plans or deeds devastated her. Whatever, she wasn't the only culprit out there...

"Talk to me," Debbie begged in tears, "and please forgive me, darling..."

Finally, the name was uttered.

Rage turned into fury, anguish into resolution. The gun in the chest of drawers flashed to her mind... She had to make up for the wrong done.

Ryan grew sanguine on learning she'd never wed him, "So he told you, I was sure of it," he yelled, "Seems that killing him hasn't been enough and now he's doing his best to keep you away from me, but I won't allow it."

Then he snatched her arm, "Listen, baby, Barry's stone dead, he'll never come back in the way you've loved him, the worms might have finished their job by now, marry me and forget him once and for all."

"I hate you, Ryan, you have damned us all," she cried, extracted the gun from her pocket and fired.

A beastly groan resounded and blood spurted from the wound.

She watched it flow out of the agonized body and rejoiced.

Being doomed to the eternal flames didn't frighten her; her final, however tardive, act of love for Barry would assure their afterlife together even if in the hellish pit.

# Neon Fly (S J Townend)

The swarm of fluorescent-green flies hovers above Mother's head as she's taken for cremation by the army. She's buckled over in pain, her guts are being digested from the inside out. I can smell the rot from her through the transparent wall that separates us: putrescine, cadaverine, death's call. A web of foamy green plaque carrying chunks of congealed blood is creeping, spreading out from the rot that has perforated her bowels. A time ago, I would've shielded Eden's eyes from such a sight, but my child has seen it all before. We're all damaged goods now, even those of us who are clean.

Dry-eyed, Mother looks up, her face nearly unrecognisable and mouths the only words left that need to be said: "I love you. Look after Eden." I blow a kiss at my mother, pull a little harder on Eden's hand and walk a little faster in the other direction.

I'm not going to cry—I genuinely feel no urge to anymore. I feel relief instead; my poor mother is going to be put out of her misery in just a few moments. The cull has been going on for so long now that the nation's tears are spent.

We stomp past the organic fruit snack stall. I see my daughter eyeing up the fresh pineapple fingers, the slices of rich red watermelon and the deep orange carrot batons. "We'll eat on the ship," I tell her and beckon her onwards.

Over the years, the majority of the world's population have chosen to lead a lifestyle consisting of poor quality food choices and so, like the ocean and the soils on planet Earth, their bodies have become riddled with nano-plastics. Microscopic pieces of polyethylene, PVC and Styrofoam have accumulated in the intestines of anyone with a less than perfect organic diet.

There was a trend, for a while, a hundred years or so back, for people to pool all of their plastics inside of a large, emptied plastic bottle. People collected these 'eco-bricks' and built walls and garden dens with them, but these mummified pseudo-environmental projects became fast submerged beneath soils and created reservoirs rich in accumulated poisons which leached and drained into nearby arable land. This all of course magnified the scale of Earth's plastics problem. A fine noxious snow of plastic soon dusted over everything and became bio-accumulated within everything, riddling everything: soil, water, most of our food and most of our people.

Bacteria modified by scientists to break these plastics down had proven successful to a degree in the oceans, but the same genetically modified microbes are unfortunately also drawn to the motes of plastic that saturate ninety-nine percent of the population's innards. Once inside the human body or the body of any living organism, they start to consume the plastic and also the flesh, gnawing their way out. They've become nicknamed the 'Piranha' bacteria. Untreatable by antibiotics which became ineffective and obsolete decades ago, once infected, a painful death shortly follows, as does the tell-tale ring of neon greenfly which headdress the infected like an emerald Renaissance era halo crown.

Oceans, lakes, rivers, have all become green. All waterways are now caked in thick sludge and stink of rot and decay as all life within them perishes. Flies—green, neon lights in the night—swarm everywhere, hovering over the freshly deceased and the not so freshly deceased, feeding, laying eggs, spreading their repulsive maggots. A stench worse than a butcher's neglected trashcan hangs thick, everywhere, so much so that survivors have almost become immune to the pungent odour. We all wear scarves over our face when we brave the outdoors.

It didn't take long for nature to mutate, to accommodate the man-made bacteria. A food chain developed fast with humans kicked down to the bottom. The novel bacteria rampaging in most people's guts, eating the plastic and then devouring the human host from inside out, became the prime food stuff of a mutant phosphorescent greenfly. Where one is found, the other follows. The contaminated wear the neon-greenfly halo of imminent death.

"I love you," I shout back from the other side of the Perspex screen which stretches sky-high like the Tower of Babel, but rather than separating people by race or language, it keeps those contaminated by poor diet and plastic and bacteria and neon fly from people like Eden and I, the organic fed.

"This way, madam." A guard hurries us into the tunnel which leads toward the interplanetary screening zone. I know we'll pass, myself and Eden. I've known since I was weaned that what we put into our mouth is what we become. I turned down plateful after plateful of food as a child, knowing that my mother had been cutting corners, dishing up processed meats, offal, cheaply farmed nutrient-depleted vegetables. I turned it all down. The thought of the disasters she used to serve up each evening still turn my stomach over now. She would send me unfed to my room, cursing me for refusing to eat the meals she'd toiled arduously over as she scraped the contents of the plate she'd dished up for me onto her own. But I knew it was all bad.

I left home as soon as I could and raised Eden in a commune. We still visited Mother and stayed at her house, but we never ate her food. Our cooperative of like-minded thinkers, farmers and eco-warriors worked our patch of land organically. We ate sparsely, but we ate well. There were no shreds of plastic in our bodies; nothing for the bacteria and the flies that followed to feast upon. When we received the letter from the World Government inviting us onto Rocket 23, I was hopeful for a better future for myself and my daughter, hopeful that perhaps some of the other barefoot children Eden had grown up with, had pulled snails and slugs from the organic lettuces and radishes with, would be on board too. Who knows where we'll end up once we land. We don't even know how many people are being sent.

Before the bacteria started to digest us, before the neon fly came, the World Government's plans for shipping out the rich, the elite, the leaders and their families from our polluted planet had been kept secret, but the truth had eventually spilled. As the neon fly had spread, world leaders spoke out, confirming the Mars Escape conspiracy. The government had been terra-forming Mars for decades.

Many of those that'd been on the elite list to be ejected from Earth in a light-speed rocket had already perished from the green plaque, or, like mother, had been found to be infected and had been pushed alive into funeral pyres which pumped dirty, green-black smoke into Earth's increasingly fucked atmosphere.

And so, with the decimation of the elite, the invitation to escape to Mars had opened up to civilians.

Any civilian that passed a series of tests were to be given the chance to be shipped out, to help colonize the red planet, to help the human race start afresh. If civilians, like myself and Eden, can prove that we aren't contaminated, that we are clean of plastic, bacteria and neon fly, then, we too can qualify as seeds for a place in one of the twenty-three rockets being launched this week.

***

"Mummy, I'm hungry." Eden is squeezing my hand. She didn't even shed a tear when her grandmother was led away for combustion. I'm so glad we are leaving this planet. "Can I get something out of the bag?"

"Not now, Eden." I'm pulling my entire belongings along behind me in a wheeled flight case. One wheel is squeaking loudly on each revolution. It was annoying as we traipsed from our home to the launch port, but now it's the least of my concerns. Now, it's drowned out by the noise of all the other anxious voices babbling around us, all the other hopefuls. Eden is pulling hers along behind us too. "There's food onboard. We just need to get through the checks."

I pick up the pace. The remnants of the World Government say there are enough spaces for all the uncontaminated, but I don't believe a word, and our seats are in the last rocket. I want to make sure we get on that damn spaceship. Barging past the other civilians, I can see the first check point directly ahead. There, we will be examined medically for any signs of the green plaque. At the second check point, our IQ will be tested. Academic limits have been placed on those seeding the red planet. We are to be re-homed up there in living quarters with our equivalents. I've forewarned Eden of this, told her to dumb things down a little, but I can tell she's fearful of lying and that she is petrified of the whole process ahead of us, because when she's nervous, she gets hungry.

*** 

I struggle to remember when I last took painkillers at the physical interrogation and the lady

41

assessing me flicks a look over to a more senior member of the investigation squad. I panic—I can't not get on this ship. We can't. To stay would be to perish, for certain. I make something up, pluck a date from thin air, which seems to placate her and she taps the information into her electronic device. How are they going to check anyway? Could they check? My heart revs, a wave of sickness shoots up my gullet. To be found lying is instant dismissal from the seeding project. She waves us through to the next investigation panel.

We smash the physical and head towards the second checkpoint but the crowd thickens as we approach it. I lose Eden for about ten minutes. This time feels like hours and I can feel myself breaking into a sweat as I push through the throngs of hopefuls, in search of my six-year-old. Where is Eden? She is always by my side, we even share a bed. For her not to be there feels like a limb is missing. I search hard, asking every person who will make eye contact with me, and find her slouched down against a wall.

Her bag is open. Its contents are poking out, a multitude of colours, like the green and red guts which splayed from Father when we found him in the yard a month back. I was left with no choice but to call Pest Control to have him exterminated.

"Thank God, Eden. I thought I'd lost you," I say and grab and hug my child and check her, over in the way a mother does, wiping her curls from her eyes, pressing her cheek against my bosom. She's all that I have left in this world, and the next. She smells so sweet. The softness of her hair comforts me but she pulls away with a look of guilt on her face.

"What's wrong?" I ask.

"Nothing, Mummy. I thought... I thought I'd lost you. I was so hungry and scared— "

"Hold my hand," I say. "We just need to clear the second gate and then we're through to interplanetary passport control." Her body language is singing to me like an out of tune piano. Everything is there in the right place, arms, legs, black and white keys, but all is not how it should be. I want to ask her more questions but the large signs mounted every hundred metres along the channel we are being herded down is telling me we simply don't have time for small talk. I will not miss this rocket. We will not miss this opportunity.

I reach for and rub my passport which I can feel underneath the skin of my upper arm. It contains a lifetime's worth of history and evidence and documentation which will allow us to embark on our new lives, up there, on that small red dot which is nearly invisible from Earth—not because it's daytime, but because clouds of green-grey pollution have made a hazy, indecipherable mess of Earth's sky. Am I making the right decision? I remind myself of the list I drafted which I left behind on the house I no longer own. I know the contents of the list off by heart. It consists of two columns, 'reasons to stay' and 'reasons to go'. The 'reasons to stay' column contains only one bullet point: 'Mother may recover', but I know that by now, Mother will be nothing more than hot white ash and dust.

***

BANG. BANG.

We both freeze. I crank my head back to locate the source of the sound and spot an armed guard, a rifle still in his hand. I grab my daughter's head and force her with me down and onto the floor behind a row of fixed seating. We huddle in silence, entwined with each other and the handles of our luggage cases.

"It's the army," I whisper in her ear, stroking her hair out from her eyes once more. She's shaking. They don't normally use guns to assassinate the contaminated—too messy.

"Security breach attempt," the guard shouts to the silenced hall. "We've shot the runner. Man down, as you were."

We slowly stand and Eden points out the dead man about hundred feet away from us. He's lying in a marbling pool of green and red which is eking out across the floor like an inflating balloon, an expanding universe, a spreading plague. Like many disgusting things, our eyes are immediately drawn to it and repulsed by it—nature's warning. But there's nothing natural about the state of our planet and the behaviour of those who deem themselves in charge of it in these desperate times.

"How did he make it through the first check?" she asked me.

"No idea," I reply. "I guess there is always the risk that someone might try and break through, to get on board. Someone contaminated but desperate enough to see Mars before they die."

"But they would bring the flies with them. It could infect our new home." I see panic in my daughter's eyes. Real worry; the whites of her eyes haunt me.

"It's not contagious though darling. Not if people stay well, eat well, treat Mars well. Hopefully the flies and the Piranha bacteria will all become a distant memory; a nightmare we can all forget about in time."

"Like Earth. Like how we can forget about Earth?"

"Yes. Like Earth."

We make it through the final gates, through the air lock and onto Rocket 23. I smile with just my mouth at Eden. I look away. I know she can almost read my mind when she really sees me through my eyes. "We've made it," I say, trying to sound as positive as I can, but I know she can sense the trepidation in my words. I'm not even sure I believe myself anymore.

An official directs one hundred or so of us through to a seated area where we belt up for take-off. The air is conditioned, the decor, economical. Eden nabs a window seat—a small oval eye, one of perhaps two hundred in total from which we can both see out from. I tell her to wave goodbye to Earth as we rise up, into, and through the clouds, as we break the ionosphere and pierce into space, as we leave the pull of our wasted planet's gravity behind. Goodbye home, goodbye roots, goodbye first love. Goodbye Mother. Goodbye Mother Earth.

"Farewell Earth," Eden says with a wave of tiny fingers and I reach over to see it off too. Good riddance.

The concrete launch pad becomes a curve of grey. The curve of grey becomes an arc of sludge-green. The sludge-green becomes a distant, ruined dot, encapsulated by a fuzzy neon green halo. The once-blue oceans found in photographs of Earth taken from space are no longer present. It is truly now just a green planet.

We sit quietly, as like our tears, most of our thoughts and questions about our relocation have already been shared.

\*\*\*

A light flashes above our heads instructing us that we're free to unbuckle, to move around the civilian floor of the rocket.

"Shall we find the food hall?" I say, trying to find the positives in the journey which lies ahead of us.

"I'm not hungry," Eden replies.

"You were starving earlier," I say. Her eyes are avoiding mine. I notice a sprinkling of crumbs decorating the corners of her mouth. "What have you been eating?" I whisper, yet my words of air are blowing through my lips like rocket-plume.

"Sorry, Mummy." Tears are collecting in the corners of her eyes. Tears I thought I'd never see again. "Earlier, when I thought I'd lost you, I opened the packet of biscuits that Grandma gave me last year. I packed them as a memory of her, even though you told me never to eat them. I was so scared—so scared and so hungry."

A pulse of vomit rises up into my throat. I don't recall ever allowing Mother to ply my child with junk. How dare she go behind my back and give my child plastic riddled shit! All these years I have been bending over backwards to provide a better life for my daughter. A healthier, safer life, a living life. I curse Mother aloud as more tears spill down Eden's cheeks. Through the window behind her, I see a red ball in the distance growing larger. The timer on the screen at the front of our compartment is telling us that our new home is under an hour away. I wipe the crumbs from my daughter's lips and pull her in tight to my chest.

"It's okay. It's okay, love. I'm sorry for being angry with you. How many did you eat?"

"The whole packet," she whispers back.

It's at this point I notice a red neon fly hovering by my daughter's ear.

And another.

And another.

\*\*\*

First published in CHLOROPHOBIA by GHOST ORCHID PRESS (2021)

# Judge's Decision (Rickey Rivers Jr.)

The judges had voted. The decision was that Hayden would be the one to represent Earth in the First Annual Planetary Beauty Pageant. Her mother was most excited of all, more so than Hayden herself. The vote came soon after Hayden had defeated forty nine other girls in the Miss Young Diva Beauty Pageant.

For this upcoming event Hayden would compete against girls from all corners of the galaxy. First place prize ensured absolute immunity against planetary destruction. Second place prize ensured only fifty percent of the population would decrease. Third place ensured a decrease of twenty five percent. Every other corner of the galaxy would have to deal with those who decided the rules, the judges, they who decided all, beings from another place, origin unspoken.

Presently, she and her mother were in training, taking time off school for the occasion.

Hayden, Miss Young Diva herself, walked crooked in high heels on the homemade platform constructed of wooden beams and bricks.

Training had to be outside, as her perfume was too strong for indoors. The lavender scent was something she was made to get used to. Possibly the judges would liken the smell? This was something her mother believed to be true.

"Who doesn't like lavender?" she had said.

The scent had to be pleasant for them who were unbiased, them who would ultimately decide the fate of all, them who had first 'suggested' the pageant.

"Steady now, Hayden," said her mother. "As you know this is a very important event, the most important!"

Hayden didn't say a word, she balanced herself, one foot in front of the other, the red, white and gold dress flowing, the crown balanced on her head, her mouth fixed in a smile unnatural. With rosy cheeks, bright red lipstick, arched eyebrows, eye shadow, painted nails and a padded bra, she was the very definition of 'the works.' Completely human yes, but to the untrained eye quite doll-like in appearance. The image of perfection, Cinderella-like, artificial exterior, a young girl with responsibility surpassing that of the president, this little one had the fate of the world on her shoulders.

"Chin up, back straight!" her mother shouted. "Eyes forward. Don't look at me. Look at the audience, wave to the judges."

And Hayden did as told, twirling herself, strutting back and forth across the platform. She pictured the judges eying her, members of the audience undressing her with their eyes. A feat that would not have taken much thought as the attires worn were meant to be revealing.

First would be casual wear, then the evening gowns, then the bathing suits. Finally, the show of talent would come, the thing that Hayden dreaded the most. Because what could that possibly entail? What worthwhile talent did she have?

Consider her competitors: the girl from Mars with multi colored skin and transparent eyes, the girl from Venus with no skin and bones like gelatine, the girl who was hair and only hair from Jupiter, the Mercury girl with teeth and eyes as her attracting feature because only that was discernible, the slimy paper thin girl of Saturn, the small green oblong shaped girl of Uranus, the Neptune girl who came encased in a glass like material, once opened revealing herself to be purely sand able to form herself into a girl shaped puzzle, the girl from Earth's Moon who had claws and fangs and beautiful silk like skin, the girl who appeared from a black hole who would not name the planet she represented because the speaking of such would cause vomiting and bleeding from the ears. Instead she had to write in her entry and even that had to be deciphered. These were only some of the girls who would compete. What of the places without names, inhabitants only recently discovered?

Amongst them all with the human skin and the human hair would be her, representing Earth, Hayden Rose, fleshy and plain.

Had the other girls been forced to diet so strictly? Were they also told to look their most attractive? She wondered if her training was in some way different than the others. Considering places of origin, their training, at least the nature of such must differ in same way, even if slight. It made sense but she thought no further of it. The idea of 'training' elsewhere scared her. Instead of fear she counted blessings.

"All right Hayden, break time," said her mother.

Hayden stopped cold and dropped her head; a sad clown, a sardonic smile frozen on her aching face. Her breathing stuttered and anxiety hung overhead as a noose.

"Not too long a break," said her mother. "Gotta make sure you stay sharp."

Hayden stood still and began to sniffle, clenching the sides of her dress. Her mother heard the sound and hated it.

"What are you doing? Stop that!"

But Hayden couldn't control what was happening. The tears began to flow from her as if they were something normal.

"Your mascara is running. Stop it right now!"

And Hayden began to mumble something very quiet and small, as a dying toy would utter a familiar phrase that had now become weak.

"What?" Her mother came closer to her. "What is it, Hayden?"

Hayden couldn't control her speech. Her tongue became a tentacle slapping around the inside of her mouth. "M-m-m."

"What is it?"

"M-mom."

"What? What is it, Hayden?!"

"I m-miss my friends. M-mom, I want to go back to school."

Her mother sighed. "Now honey, you know you can't do that. Without you here doing what you're doing, school might not exist at all."

"My friends-"

"Them too, you don't want them to suffer, right?"

Hayden shook her head.

"Don't you want to please Mommy?"

She nodded.

"Don't you want to save the world?"

She nodded again.

"Then this is what you have to do. We've been over this before. You're the one the judges voted for. You were so happy about that before, so proud of it."

"I-I don't know how I can compete against aliens."

"What do you mean? Is that a lack of confidence I hear?"

"No. I-"

"Are you not more beautiful than them? Not pleasantly shaped? For goodness sake, honey, you've inherited Mommy's figure. Of course you can win!"

"Mom, I don't want to do this anymore. It was fun before. This isn't fun. My feet hurt. My neck hurts. The dress itches."

"Hayden Ryan Rose, you listen to your mother."

"Yes, ma'am."

"You need to stop being selfish and think about the people of Earth. How many people you're going to be letting down if you don't go through with this. This is important. We're talking about the whole planet, the fate of humanity."

"I know, Mom."

"Do you? Do you really understand the gravity of the situation?"

"I-I think so."

"Now you only think so. Well, I think it's time we get back to training. Dry your eyes, breaks over."

"Mom-"

"Eyes forward, back straight, chin up, smile wide for the people!"

Hayden dried her eyes and did as told. Walking and twirling and smiling and waving. She added a curtsy to the routine and her mother enjoyed that.

"Oh yes, that will drive the judges wild. Keep that, I like it! The other girls can't compete."

All the while Hayden let her body move, her mind was in a distant place. She became robotic and unknowing of her surroundings. A windup toy, because only her body was there in the backyard. Only her body mattered. Her mind was simply thinking, considering, wondering: was this to be tradition? Were the judges to return the following year and so forth? She couldn't know. She dared not consider the possibility of winning and having to compete again, year after year. It would break her. She understood that. At this point, she was almost broken anyway.

Something came to her. It slid into her mind as a serpent. Only three things became clear, three choices to choose from. Choice one: go on with the pageant, give it her best shot and hopefully win it. Choice two: take her life and let the judges' vote on a suitable replacement. And Choice three: throw the pageant and watch the Earth go down in a fiery blaze of glory.

How could she consider when every choice seemed to be right? Each one had its allure. Each would please and hurt at least one person. The weight of it all became a crushing thing, a burden. She beneath it all, beneath the universe, hair a mess and dressed crumpled. A broken doll, laying there, the bodies of her friends and family among others above her, disappointed moments before death.

Someone or something would pass her by and say "What a pretty dress" in their own language, as they look down at the doll who used to be a girl who used to be normal and happy. The doll's makeup smeared from the tears, spread across her face so sloppy you'd think she was a clown. Used, directed by the ringmaster, surrounded by the circus of it all.

"That's it, honey, keep smiling!"

And smile she did the whole time. At this point her face had gotten used to the expression. Wound up, her body moving on its own, twirling and prancing, her mind mechanic and all the while considering the choice. Quite a decision for a doll, to decide the fate of the doll maker, the doll factory and every other factory, but she had that power.

Alternatively, would a clown ever decide to ruin the whole circus? Would that be fair to everyone else? And which was she really, a clown, a doll or a clown doll? Whichever one could fit; but no, Hayden was human.

So, what choice would she make? Not only for the fate of humanity but for herself. Which made the most sense? Only she would know, until they all did. She would stand in front of them with a plan in her head and a twinkle in her eye. Hayden Ryan Rose, age eleven.

"Hayden! Are you listening?" Her mother was screaming. Hayden wondered if she'd ever hear that scream again, would it be more stressful in unison.

"Yes, Mother," said Hayden, clenching her teeth. "I'm listening."

"Good!" And her mother's direction went on, standing so proud in front of her daughter.

And Hayden went on to do as instructed, until she made her decision.

# Radium Cigarettes (Gary Budgen)

At Liverpool Street Station the rolling advertising posters display the smooth flanks of luxury cars next to the smooth flanks of women lounging amid palm trees and sun-block bottles. Then, like a bony hand on my shoulder those adverts, those well-meant solicitations become a demand to donate to cancer, dementia and heart disease.

I crossed Bishopsgate quickly into Artillery Lane and that obscure neighbourhood of backstreets that had somehow escaped the waves of redevelopment.

The shop had a dusty window display behind a metal grill but none of us in the know ever looked in the window at all that popular trash. No, the treasures we were after were elsewhere.

The spring bell on the top of the door sounded as I entered. I could hear a familiar voice down the book filled aisles.

"…suppose with the internet a lot of the trade's gone, people buying online. You should be doing that. Put a whole new lease of life in the business…"

I followed the voice deeper into the shop. Fred sat behind the counter, hidden by a huge grey monitor from the cathode ray era. Callum Kelly was talking and looming over him, black curls shaking as he talked, scruffy as always in his long Afghan coat and sandals.

"…and," he went on, "the online business feeds back and sustains the bookshop…"

There was desperation in Kelly's brash tone. He didn't want the shop to close down.

From the other side of the monitor came the sound of a match being struck and then a column of smoke rose up.

"I've made up my mind," came Fred's phlegmy voice.

"But Fred…" Kelly began before Fred stopped him by calling out.

"Who's that? Come in."

"Oh," said Kelly, "It's only Garth."

Fred coughed and stood up, a cloud of cigarette smoke moving with him.

"Hello, Garth. Glad you've come."

"Maybe you can change his mind," Kelly said to me.

There was something about Fred's face emerging from the smoke which told me it was no good. Fred saw me glance off to the left and the aisle that led to the back of the shop and a locked door. Where the treasures were.

"Why don't we all have a little drink?" Fred said, "Drag some chairs over."

There were folding chairs positioned around the shop, in corners, in aisles. Some held piles of books. Soon Kelly and I were sat on the other side of the counter to Fred who pushed the monitor over as far as he could, giving himself a minor coughing fit. He produced a bottle of vodka and paper cups from the below the counter.

The bell on the door sounded.

"Ah," said Fred, "now we are complete. Hello Miranda, come and join us."

Miranda's small frame always seemed lost in the folds of baggy clothing, feet sticking out in her enormous DM boots. Today she had her dark hair tucked up almost completely in a woollen beret.

"What's this?" she said as I gave up my chair to her and began to look for another, "Started the party without me."

"The last supper," said Fred and made a noise between a cough and a laugh.

I fetched another chair from topography.

"Well," said Miranda after she'd taken a good slosh of vodka, "Why are you closing down, Fred?"

"The internet," said Kelly.

"No," said Fred, scowling at him, He took another drink.

"Someone priced you out?" I said, "Property developers?"

He laughed. "Property developers... Made me an offer I couldn't refuse. Not quite... not quite. Very smart, no cheap estate agents suits. No. I'd been investigating them. Seen what they are up to. They don't like that, no they don't like that."

"Who are you talking about?" I asked.

He waved this away.

"Let' drink," he said.

I looked at him, his haggard face. Had he crossed some imperceptible line into paranoia?

We drank more, talked about a shared past revolving around similar evenings drinking after hours, laughing at eccentric customers.

"Well," Fred eventually announced, "Our revels are ended. Off with you all. Come back tomorrow. It'll be calmer here tomorrow."

\*\*\*

The next day I went to the shop where a van had somehow squeezed down the tiny street. A man in overalls came out of the shop carrying a cardboard box. I went inside. Another man in overalls was sweeping books off shelves with little care and packing them into the boxes.

"What's going on?" I said.

Miranda appeared.

"Fred's sold all the stock. Paperwork is in order."

I glanced towards the back, towards the locked room.

"Oh no," she said, "Apparently what's in the back room is for us. I've rung Kelly. I think we should wait for him."

"Okay. Where's Fred?"

"He's gone. The upstairs flat's empty."

Kelly came in out of breath, hair even wilder than usual. He hardly glanced about him at the nearly empty shop or at the men in overalls.

"I've been followed," he said.

Was Kelly trying to make it all about him? But no, he was actually shaking.

"A man... I don't know. He was looking at me."

"It's all right, Cal," said Miranda, "It's okay."

Kelly looked at us both.

"He was beautiful," he said.

The two workmen were looking over, amusement on their faces.

"Come on," I said, "Let's go into the back room. See what Fred's left for us."

Kelly looked over his shoulder, out past the empty shelves. The workmen were now outside smoking.

"Sure," he said.

I got the keys out and we all went to the back of the shop. Our little coterie was over now; the shop had been what had held it together. I focused on what I hoped to find in the back room, rare books Fred had hinted he'd kept for years.

I opened the door and I turned on the light to particles of dust floating in the air.

The bookshelves were empty. There was some sort of box on the Formica table in the middle of the room. The book shelf against the back wall had been pulled forward to reveal a door to a yard I'd not known was there.

On the table I saw that what was there was a box file. On the top was a slip of paper taped on with Sellotape. Written on the paper was: Garth.

We went to a yard hemmed in by the walls of buildings. Grass grew between the paving stones. Against the wall were bits of junk, nails, broken tines of a garden fork, and cans of liquid fertilizer. Perhaps Fred had been a very optimistic gardener.

"I think I'm going to go," said Miranda.

"What's in the box?" said Kelly.

"Fred left it for Garth," said Miranda.

60

"It's all right," I said, even though I was reluctant to share any last secret. "Let's go inside and look."

The workmen had gone from the shop. The books, the computer, even the chairs had gone. We stood around the counter. I opened the box file and picked up an object from on top of the paperwork.

It was a vintage metal cigarette tin. A BATSCHARI. CIGARETTES. RADIUM. There was a white sun in the centre which contained a pyramid with three letters in circles. A. B. C. Red sun rays spread out across a blue background.

Miranda took it from me and threw it back into the box file, then closed the lid.

"I'm going," she said. "Good luck with that lot, Garth."

"I'll walk with you," said Kelly. He was suddenly wary. Not wanting to be on his own.

"We should keep in touch," I said.

"Why?" said Kelly.

Miranda shrugged, nodded.

Then I was alone in the emptied shop. I locked everything up and walked away with my inheritance.

*** 

Typewritten pages from what appeared to have been a diary or journal. No dates or page numbers and not stacked in any order. Newspaper clippings on diverse, possibly even random, subjects.

And the radium cigarettes. Or rather, the tin, since it was empty, the cigarettes long ago turned to ash on the ground and the smoke drawn deep into black lungs.

A flavour of the newspaper clippings.

The Ikea riot of 2005 when the Edmonton store had opened and thousands of shoppers had stampeded in to get bargains. Fights ensued about sofas. Twenty people were hospitalized.

Profiles of various TV personalities, newsreaders, weather forecasters. For example a vacuous lifestyle piece about a popular singer where she talked about her difficult childhood which seemed to exist in a storybook world, how this early life somehow made her surprising fame deserved. There were details about her favourite places to shop and to eat, what she liked to wear.

A journal entry by Fred.

Outside Liverpool Street Station, a perfect spring morning, the commuter hordes should have cleared by the time I got there but I saw a crowd had gathered, all staring up at a large television screen I hadn't noticed before. Although no-one was talking, there was a palpable sense of excitement. I thought at first something momentous had happened. On the screen was someone standing on a stage, a countdown on the corner of the screen. The person on the stage was saying something. He wore a white suit, open collared, purple shirt, no necktie. He was smugly healthy. The countdown approached zero, the people in the crowd began to take out mobile phones and take pictures of the screen.

I approached a woman at the edge of the crowd, holding her phone up. I asked what was happening.

She didn't look at me as she spoke of the launch of a new version of some phone or other.

She shushed me as the man on the screen began speaking.

"With its new sleek lines it will take you into the future…"

I walked away, sickened, went back to the shop, intending to lock myself in the back room and read something that might drive all this away. But all I could do was sit at the counter. I held the radium cigarettes in my hand.

There were others accounts of Fred's wanderings around London, noticing strange accumulations of people into crowds attending product launches, sales and celebrity appearances.

If he was making some point about the alienation of modern life, it was overdone.

I googled A BATSCHARI.

German cigarette manufacturer. Their own fan web page. History of the company etc. They employed well-known graphic designers of the time to produce their branding, product packaging and advertising. Many of these items, such as the posters and signs, the cigarettes packets themselves were now highly collectible. Examples of a stylish art-deco era of yesteryear.

"During the period of radioactive quackery in the early $20^{th}$ century, Batschari also produced a brand of radium radioactive cigarettes."

After the discovery of radium there were great claims for its beneficial health benefits and it was used in many products. The effects were generally disastrous as long term exposure to radium can lead to anaemia, cataracts, fractured teeth, cancer and death.

*\*\**

Days must have passed sitting at the kitchen table, the contents of the box file spread out on it. I thought of calling Miranda but what would I tell her? that Fred Diablo, our cantankerous yet clubbable old bookshop owner, had gone down a rabbit hole in pursuit of an obsession I didn't understand.

Then Miranda called me.

"Something's happened to Kelly," she said.

"Kelly?" I tried to keep the disappointment out of my voice, "What?"

"Look," she sounded - not worried, not precisely. Rather there was a hint of bemusement in her voice. "It's easier if you just see, meet me, will you?"

I wanted to see her under whatever circumstance so we agreed to meet at Liverpool Street. She was very precise about the time, just before one o'clock.

The train was a few minutes late. Miranda was waiting outside the platform gates and grabbed hold of my arm, pulling me along.

"Come on," she said, "we have to get there before one o'clock or we'll miss him."

"What's going on?"

"You'll see…"

We rushed out of the station and through the narrow streets beneath the shadow of the tower blocks. At last we stopped in the back doors of a building. Across the street was one of those typical office block entrances, a glass façade with revolving doors built into it. I could see a reception desk with a concierge.

"What is this place?" I asked.

"I've no idea."

"Well, then, why…?"

"Watch. Kelly's always on time. Like a bird out of a clock."

A few people came out of the building, men and women in office suits, some chatting to one another.

"Lunch time," she announced.

"Miranda?"

"There. There he is." She nodded across the road.

"Who?"

But then I saw him. Like all the others he wore a business suit. His wild hair had been cut and was now a neat layer of short curls. He walked with the crowd, the quick step of those on the clock, heading for some sandwich bar or café.

"Kelly?" I was incredulous.

"Come on," she said, "You should talk to him."

We trotted to catch up and Miranda tapped Kelly on his shoulder.

He turned and looked at us both. Then his eyes shifted away.

"Oh," he said, "It's you again."

His voice was flat. He looked through us. Not catching our eyes.

"How are you, Kelly?" she asked.

"I'm fine. It's nice bumping into you like this after all this time. But I really have to get on."

"Hello, Kelly," I said.

"Yes. Hello."

He turned his head towards me but wasn't really looking at me.

"It's…" he wagged a finger. "It's Garth. Yes. It's been a long time."

"What do you mean, a long time?"

He ignored this and looked at his watch. Even I could recognize it as an expensive model.

"Well," he said, "I must be going."

And he walked off to get his lunch.

"What's happened to him?"

"Well," said Miranda, "whatever happened it was almost overnight. One minute he was talking about being stalked, really freaking out. He said it was people like the one he'd seen on the way to the shop that last day. I was beginning to think he'd had a full scale breakdown. Then he packed up and left my flat."

"Your flat?"

"He'd moved in… Crashing on the sofa… Anyway he was flighty… didn't want to stay in his house down by the river. He said he had started to see them whenever he was out walking. I made him take me with him once and he'd freak out at some figure in the distance and turn back the other way. I tried to tell him it was just some random bloke. An average normal person. He wouldn't have it. So he came to stay with me. Then he was gone."

"But he hardly seemed to recognize me."

"Yes," she said, "It was like that with me. I followed him from his house. When I spoke to him it was like he hadn't seen me in years."

We rationalized it. He had indeed had a breakdown. Or was on drugs. Or like a lot of trust fund kids had suddenly got bored with slumming it and decided to join the world he'd always professed to despise. This whole thing of hardly recognizing us was some variety of cognitive dissonance, his way of coping with discarding his old life.

Neither of us believed what we were saying. We fell into silence and Miranda said she should be going. I didn't want her to leave. It felt as though this was the final disintegration of the old crowd. But I couldn't think of anything to say that would keep her.

On the way to catch my train I saw a crowd gathering. They were staring up at the giant TV screen and I thought of what Fred had written. The people were hardly talking. Row on row of suited City workers. They might have been participants in one of those mass weddings the Moonies perform. I stood at the back of the crowd and looked up at the screen. The sound was off but a banner of text commentary ran across the bottom.

A man had entered the exhibition centre at Olympia during the Gadget Show. He had rushed towards the stage of some presentation by a minor celebrity and blown himself up with a homemade nail bomb. The bomber had died along with the celebrity and several exhibition goers. It was a senseless, brutal, act.

I was about to walk away, to do what we all do after such acts that don't directly affect us: initiate a process that would mean we'd forgotten about it within a few weeks. Then Fred Diablo's face appeared, caught in a moment of CCTV footage. I assumed he was one of the victims.

Then the text identified him as the bomber.

My legs gave way. I might have fallen, I definitely vomited. I had to lean against the nearest wall. I tried to pull myself together and telephoned Miranda but her phone went to voicemail. I stared back at the crowd, at their faces raised to the screen. Bathed in its flickering light, those faces expressed only a bland, choreographed, outrage. Soon each of them would post a social media status about the incident, then drift into comforting amnesia. I walked back through the streets where I overheard people talking. The bomb wasn't mentioned and I found it hard to follow the snippets of conversation which seemed to be allusions to brand names, reports of shopping trips, the sex lives of actors and pop stars.

\*\*\*

I'd tried to ring Miranda again but without success. I tried at least once a day for a few days and then gave up.

The more I wanted to make sense of it all the more it eluded me. Reference to the bombing in the media almost disappeared and when it was mentioned at all the focus had shifted. One of the security guards who'd been only slightly injured had won a contract as the face of a new brand of after shave. There was a big feature on the refurbishment of the damaged Olympia site. It was a fantastic regeneration opportunity, the moment for a bold new artistic statement.

Fred's papers were dotted with reference to *them*, the ubiquitous source of a malignity. But then Fred had become paranoid, caught in a web of delusion that didn't even have the virtue of most conspiracy theories of being internally consistent. And it had turned him into a monster.

I would end each night staring at all his papers and clippings along with the new notes I had added myself. A bottle of wine would have been emptied. I would hold the tin of radium cigarettes in my hand.

*** 

One evening the agents finally came. They never identified themselves. I thought of them as agents rather than police officers. Two men in their thirties wearing expensive suits. Their faces were angled and perfectly proportioned, without a blemish. The savage glint in their eyes made them seem capable of anything. They were beautiful.

They came in without invitation and told me to sit on my sofa. One sat opposite me in the armchair, the other wandered around the room, looking at bookshelves, examining the TV, the stereo.

"So," said the seated one, "You were an associate of Fred Dransfield, the bookseller."

I had never heard that surname but it didn't matter. I nodded.

"You were part of the cell that met in the bookshop. Can we assume you knew about what he was planning to do?"

"No," I said. "Absolutely not."

There was a narrative being established here, one I could see leading me to places I did not want to be.

The walking agent looked over at me.

"He's terrified," he said, laughed for a moment then went out of the room. I heard him ascending the stairs with steady even steps.

"I had nothing to do with it," I said.

"What did you go to the bookshop for?"

"Well, to get books."

"What, like these?" He gestured at my bookshelves. "Why do you need all these books?"

I didn't know what to say. He'd gone off in a completely different direction to what I'd expected.

"You don't seem to have much stuff," he said. "What do you do all the time?"

The other agent came in. He had my laptop. He threw it on the sofa next to me.

"This is obsolete," he said. "Why don't you get a decent one? Give me your phone."

I got it out and he snatched it from me. Looked at it a moment and threw it next to the laptop.

"People like you disgust me…"

He was going to hammer home that I was complicit in a truly terrible act, one for which there could be no forgiveness. But that wasn't what he said at all.

"You think you're so much better than everyone else, with you little cliques and books. You can't even get yourself a decent phone or computer. Your kitchen is twenty years out of date. Look at your stuff, the old things are not even fashionably retro."

He was gripping the edge of the armchair where his colleague sat. The colleague looked around at him.

"It's all right," he said, "It's all right."

Then the seated one looked back at me.

"So, Fred Dransfield never gave you an intimation of what he intended to do?"

I was scared. That's why I did told them about the papers.

I eagerly fetched the box file and handed it over to the agent in the armchair. The other looked over his shoulder as the box was opened.

The agent took out the radium cigarettes and held up the tin. He glanced at his companion and they both smiled momentarily.

He put the cigarette tin on the arm of the chair then tipped the rest of the box file onto the floor. There lay all of Fred's clippings and notes.

He looked down at it all for a moment then stared over at me.

"You don't need to be such a loser," he said.

"It's pitiful," said the other.

Then he stood up and dusted his jacket as though he'd gotten dirty by being here. He put his foot down on the notes on the floor. It was while I was looking at his shiny shoe pressed down and smearing a stain on the papers that he palmed the cigarette tin and popped it into his jacket pocket. It was as though it had never been there at all.

*** 

Later that evening the phone rang, an unknown number.

"Is that… Garth?" It was Miranda.

"Miranda. I've been trying to talk to you for ages," I said, "You've seen what happened… with Fred… are you all right?"

There was a long pause before she answered.

"Garth…" she said at last.

"Are you okay?"

"It's been a long time."

It had been a couple of weeks.

"What's happened Miranda?"

I thought of Kelly, of the blankness of his face…

"I… Garth? It's Garth, isn't it? My God, what's happening to me? I'm trying to understand. It's like the way time flows on TV. Scenes, days apart somehow next to each other, years can pass with the shift of light on the screen…"

"Miranda?"

"I think I see it, for a moment I see it. I can hardly think. Whole afternoons looking in shop windows at things I don't really want… Everything is so beautiful, so wonderful."

There was another pause. Sometimes a wordless telephone line feels like the depths of the ocean.

"Who is this?" she said.

72

I told her.

"Garth? It's been a long time."

\*\*\*

I drink. I drift into another tense, the natural tense now. I don't go out much. I spend my time studying the notes Fred left behind for me. Everyday something has a new resonance. That the world has changed is obvious. It is trying to pinpoint what, or who is responsible that keeps me occupied.

One night, late into a second bottle of wine, I take a sheet of paper and write.

I call them the Batschari but that is not their name. Sometime in the twentieth century they started to do something to us, to poison us. I began to see them, to understand. Even as they murder us they deny death is real. As the century progressed they felt more confident to emerge. They filled the billboards by the sides of the roads, the magazine adverts, the cinema screens. Then the world of television and the computer screens.

We adore their disposable electric toothbrushes, cotton buds and coffee cups. If we were to fight them they would just turn it into a game show. If you want picture of the future imagine a product launch for something nobody really needs and yet everyone desires, imagine it going on forever.

I go one last time into central London. At Liverpool Street all the cancer and dementia posters have gone, abolished as though they had been the propaganda of a defeated resistance. Instead bright faces, irresistible bodies sell cars and holidays.

I suppose I am looking for Miranda. I think of her in smart work clothes, in high heels. I think of succumbing to the infinite lure of the products she wears. I look for her but there are people like that everywhere. Even the shop dummies might seduce me.

Artillery Lane, down the back streets and alleys, finding myself outside the bookshop or where it had been for there is now a row of shining glass-fronted units instead. There is a nail bar, a mobile phone shop, a greetings card shop. I can't tell which one had been the bookshop. There is a retro furniture store where the past has become a colony of the extended present of our new reality. In the window, amongst a display that includes an old Imperial typewriter, a nineteen fifties plastic robot and some vintage *Playboys*, I think I might find something, a small tin decorated with the symbol of the sun. But already I have forgotten what it is for and there are so many other things everywhere to look at.

# The People of the Desert (Jason R. Frei)

I was in Marrakesh on a 'study abroad' program when I received the letter from my Uncle Lucius. Details were vague, but he was greatly excited by some sort of discovery he had made. Lucius had a reputation for being eccentric, so his discovery could mean anything.

I moved to the University six years ago and in that time I had not seen much of my uncle. My parents passed when I was young and it was my uncle who took me in. Lucius inspired me to study archaeology and paleontology and it was with shared excitement that I received the news.

I say excitement, but in reality I was somewhat relieved. One of my uncle's eccentricities was of a recurring nightmare he had in which he was violently kidnapped by an unknown people and sacrificed to their deities. This nightmare remained fresh in my mind as I traveled throughout Morocco. There are rumors—hideous and grotesque rumors— of dark magic and deviant worship in the area. My studies unveiled several appalling visions that will never leave my mind and they made me think of Lucius often.

I flew back to the residence where I had grown up. The estate was roughly fifty acres covered in gardens, forested areas and flat expanses of lush green yards. An ornate Roman fountain in the front courtyard displayed a scene of Hercules with his massive hands around the jaws of the Nemean lion.

The house itself was an architectural wonder built to my uncle's exact specifications. The bottom two floors were modeled after a Spanish villa. The walls were smooth and eggshell white. The windows were large and domed, trimmed in beige-glazed tile. Balconies jutted from the second floor perfectly symmetrical with one another. Red brick stairs led up the sides of the balconies.

The top level of the building, which included the roof, was in the Gothic style. Gray and white stone slabs inter-layered in tall spires and colonnades that left the top floor open. Intricate designs wound throughout the columns. The roof was sharply angled and grotesque gargoyles lorded over each corner, their mouths open to let water stream out.

A round stained glass mural adorned the center of the roof; its grandeur could only be truly viewed by standing directly beneath it. The outer ring of the mural was embellished with strange and wondrous beasts, while the center depicted a dark purple-almost-black pyramid.

While it would seem that these two architectural styles were at odds with one another, they fitted perfectly together and with the atmosphere of the house.

I had never fully grown accustomed with the structure, either the outside or the inside. Uncle Lucius had assembled one of the world's premiere collections of artifacts from the earliest stages of humankind. He had tools dating back 250,000 years. There were several tablets from the earliest stages of language, one of which was no less than 50,000 years old. There were lead statues, clay pottery shards, carved rock fertility goddesses and dolls made out of a type of grass that disappeared thousands of years ago. It was more museum than house and there was always a backdrop of apprehension and foreboding.

When I arrived, I was met by Helena, the maid and Nirom, the butler, both of whom served Lucius for far longer than I had been his ward. Helena had been my nanny when I first came to live with Lucius. I hugged them both tight and enquired after my uncle. Nirom rolled his eyes and shrugged. He took my luggage to a bedroom suite while Helena ushered me into the kitchen for something to eat. While I ate, I plied Helena and Nirom for more answers about my uncle's cryptic note.

They both smiled and looked at each other. "You know your uncle," said Nirom. "Everything is a production."

Helena added, "He's been cooped up in his study for days. We were relieved when he sent the letter to bring you home. Perhaps you can persuade him to return to the land of the living?" Hope glimmered in her eyes.

Once I had eaten, I walked through the house, re-familiarizing myself with the layout. Lucius's collection had grown and some of the pieces looked much older and foreign than those had been here before. There were oddly colored stone effigies and tools made of a metal I had never seen. The pieces gave off an aura, one of disquietude. I touched one of the pieces: my arms broke out in gooseflesh and the hairs rose up on the back of my neck.

Some of the artifacts, besides exuding a maliced discontent, were unsettling to look at and caused uneasiness in my chest. They were both physically and psychically repugnant. On one table was a solid black tablet that showed some sort of ritual sacrifice. Beings resembling upright slugs dragged chained creatures to a pit and were in the process of throwing them in. The pit was lined with teeth and although it was just a carving, the walls of teeth seemed to undulate in waves.

With a growing feeling of unrest, I wandered further into the house and, as was usual when living here, I came at last to the library. The door creaked open and familiar scents wafted toward me - old leather book bindings, fresh vellum pages, the tang of ink. I ran my hand along the spines of the books filling every shelf from floor to ceiling.

Uncle Lucius was at his desk in his oversized leather chair. The desk was mahogany and dark stained and was more of a writing table than a desk. The wood was smooth and worn from years of use. A cigar sat smoldering in a brass ashtray.

My uncle was absorbed in whatever he was writing and had not noticed me entering the room. I cleared my throat and he looked up, somewhat dazed.

"James?" he asked my uncle with a quizzical look on his face. Then his features brightened and he leapt out of his chair. "My dear boy!"

Uncle Lucius crossed the room quickly with his long strides. He was tall and thin, his face gaunt and graying hair wisped out from his head haphazardly. Surely this was not the same man I left just six years ago. The Uncle Lucius I knew had been hale and healthy, a bit portly with thick black hair that curled at his neck.

Nevertheless, Uncle Lucius gripped me in a strong hug that lingered far longer than was usual. I wasn't sure if he was truly that glad to see me, or if he was just glad to have a grip on something real. In time, he stepped back and held me at arm's length.

"Look at you, nephew." His once-baritone and booming voice was now shaky and barely more than a whisper. "You are a sight for weary eyes."

He ushered me to a leather wingback chair and bade me sit. He handed me a brandy snifter and took one up himself then sat at the edge of his immense desk. His eyes had a faraway haunted look to them and he seemed to stare right through me.

"Uncle," I said, startling him. He looked around as if he had forgotten I was there. I pressed on. "You don't look well."

He waved his hand dismissively and took a large gulp from his glass. The previous look returned to his eyes. What was it exactly? Despair? Consternation? Fear?

I sat my glass on a side table and leaned forward. "Uncle? Why have you asked me here from my studies?"

His eyes cleared and filled with excitement. "Ah yes," he exclaimed. "What do you make of this, James?"

He reached behind him and then handed me a package wrapped in muslin. I unwrapped the covering and found a small brown journal and an odd looking dagger. This had a hilt of black rock that looked possibly volcanic in nature. There were rust-colored spots on the book.

I set the knife aside and opened the journal. It was written by a Professor Douglas Shadwell and detailed an expedition to a desert located somewhere on the borders of Europe and Asia. It spoke of a race of dark-skinned men named the Mubashi who roamed the desert nearly 500,000 years ago. Surely this was a mistake as men were not known to have lived at such an early time.

The notes were painstaking and provided details of a tribe that were beyond agriculture and farming. They had built large dwellings shaped like pyramids. The stone they used was unique to the area and I recognized the description as the same material that made the hilt of the knife. I re-examined the hilt and the rock was unusually light, but durable. While it was black and smooth like ebony, I could see no reflection in its surface.

The diary spoke of families being yoked together at birth and performing sacrifices to fuel their pyramids. They held to a belief that by sacrificing themselves, they would ascend to their place in the stars. Then they would meet their gods of old.

I suddenly became aware that I was alone in the study and that the room was very dark. The mantel clock showed that I had spent several hours in rapt attention to the writings in the journal. I pocketed it and went to the kitchen for my supper. My uncle had gone to bed. After my repose, I went to my bedroom and got ready for the night. I lit a small oil lantern on the bedside table and made myself comfortable among the silken sheets and satin comforter. Once I was situated, I opened the journal again.

I flipped to the last written page in the diary.

It is with great excitement and some trepidation that I write this. If you have read this far, then you have read my detailed notes on the Mubashi, the people of the desert. I have not only discovered where they once lived, but I believe I have found an opening to one of their pyramidal dwellings.

Whilst surveying at the base of a large dune, my hired diggers broke through a cave-like opening. Upon further inspection we discovered strange hieroglyphs on the tiled floor. We were able to bring in some portable lighting and found that the hieroglyphs extended from the floor up the walls to the ceiling itself, which was only five to six feet above our heads. While they bear some resemblance to the ancient Sumerian cuneiforms, they seem to mix in some Phoenician glyphs and even some Meroitic script from the Minoan culture of Crete. It is truly a wonderful discovery as these writings may be the basis for all other writing that developed later.

Traveling further back into the cave, we entered a small tunnel that went down at a sharp angle before opening into a cavernous room. Even with the lights we could not see the ceiling! In the center of the room was a pit, approximately ten feet across.

The sides of the pit appeared to have been chiseled very carefully as they were very smooth with no discernible notches or marks. Again, our lights could not penetrate the bottom. One of my hired men threw a stone in, but we never heard it land.

The floor was covered in crude clay tiles that seemed to have been baked long in the sun for they were quite strong. Each one showed a grouping of men with their hair tied to each other's heads. Each group was leading some large undefined beast. The tiles were situated so that each grouping was pointing directly at the pit. The tiles around the pit were vastly different than the ones on the floor. They were more carefully made and glazed with a red hue, similar to rust.

We set about collecting samples and surveying the area while several of the camels and pack horses became nervous. They were snorting and pawing at the ground. One of the camels reared backwards into the pit, pulling its handler with it. They made no noise even as they fell to their certain death. Several minutes passed until we could finally hear a sound, very small at first. It was a rhythmic sound, like a chanting. Shortly after that, a small spark rose up from the center of the pit, reflecting off the walls like a wild fire.

It was at this point that my hired men, being a superstitious lot to begin with, began to hastily gather their tools and make their way out of the cavern. I begged for them to stay, but in the end I had to abandon my studies as they took all of the lighting. Once we cleared the entrance, several of them set dynamite around its mouth and blew it shut.

I now wish that this had been the end of the expedition; however, that night, one of the men discovered a dagger in with his tools that was not his. He brought it to me immediately and stated that there was "something wrong about it". Indeed, it was an odd knife. The blade was of a metal I had never seen. It had an iridescence about it that looked like oil had been poured on and tilted around the whole blade. The hilt was of stone, not wood, and was black and glossy. The blade was unusually sharp and cut with just a gliding over any surface. The hired man showed a cut on his palm from when he picked up the dagger. The edges of the wound were fine with no jagged skin.

The dagger was cataloged and put with my collection of etchings and other small pieces that had been found. The entire team was exhausted and camp was made early. No sentries were needed as we were welcome in the desert by its Bedouin peoples.

Hours after everyone had fallen asleep, a commotion raised the camp. Three of the laborers were missing, their footprints still fresh in the sand and pointed back toward where we had come. I checked my items to make sure they would be secure when I noticed that the knife was missing. We hurried at once to follow the men, as we thought they were going back to the cavern to steal artifacts.

We were a few hundred meters from the dune when the scouts in front relayed to us that the opening was once again exposed and accessible.

The sun had just peeked over the dune when we saw a most terrible sight. The three men had stripped nude and painted themselves with blue lines, the paint still dripped wetly down their bronzed bodies. They had also bound their hair together in one massive braid.

We rushed toward them to stop their delirium, but they had a head start and went headlong into the cavern. We followed and watched in terror as they threw themselves into the pit. A few seconds later, a ball of fire shot out of the pit and went straight up. It exploded into the ceiling, revealing that the walls that high up were sloped to a point.

The fire ball hit the point and arched out over the walls, rolling down toward us. We ran out of the cavern as sparks shot all around and a thick cloud of foul-smelling smoke followed. I saw a glint in the sand several feet in front of me and reached down to retrieve the dagger that had been stolen. This time, I led the crew in detonating the entrance so that it would never again see the light of day.

I returned home swiftly after that to document my expedition; however, at this point, I believe I am becoming delirious. While cataloging the knife, its keen-edged blade slid across my thumb. It bled just a little, but the pain was more than it should have been. Since then, I have been sensing the desert in my own home. I find small piles of sand at intervals along the corridors. The smell of cinders, ash and spice wafts throughout my rooms. And just this very morning, the edges of my cut have turned an unnatural, but alluring shade of blue.

This was the end of the writing in the journal. The light in my lamp had grown low and the oil was almost gone. Although it was still dark when seen through the windows, it was becoming lighter and morning could not be far away. I got out of bed and wrapped myself in my robe. Although a feeling of dread hung over me, I was determined to find out more.

I left my room and was heading toward the library when I heard strange noises from the floor above me. I had never been fond of the third floor. Although it was open on all sides like a portico, I always felt a sort of claustrophobia. The filtered light through the dark mural threw the room into a perpetual state of gloominess. Strange shadows leapt out from behind the garden furniture and odd designs were carved into the floor and columns.

I climbed the narrow stairway to a trapdoor that opened into the center of the room. I saw a faint luminescence in the west corner even though the sun was not high enough to penetrate this space. A small breeze whipped past me bringing the scent of spices, cloying and sickeningly sweet, like saffron, cardamom and cinnamon. They masked the scent of something else, something ancient and long forgotten - the smell of funeral dust and burned flesh.

There was a sound that started small, but gradually deepened - chanting and the lowing of animals. The light flared and within it I saw what can only be described as pyramids, the numbers of which I could not count. They were purplish-black with outcroppings of a color darker than black.

They had many sides that should not have fit together, but did so at odd and unsettling angles.

The pyramids rose high above a desert floor and avenues wound between them. The chanting grew louder as streams of men led animals to the bases of the pyramids. The men were nude with skin darkened from the blazing sun in the sky. Electric blue lines etched their skin forming chaotic and discordant patterns. They marched three across, their thick, black hair braided into each other's head, keeping them more captive than the animals they led.

The animals were hulking, each one the height of five men. Their bodies were shelled and hard, like a beetle, with three pairs of segmented legs appearing from beneath the carapaces. The heads were bull-like, with longish snouts and curled horns. Four eyes shone brightly from two horizontal slits in the face, just above the snout. They snorted and huffed in an almost intelligible language.

A throng reached the base of the pyramids and I saw an opening. Wisps of smoke curled out lazily. When a grouping of men and animals entered, the smoke deepened and sparks shot out into the sky like fireworks. The pyramids seemed to blur or vibrate each time.

After an undetermined amount of time, one of the pyramids belched out thick, black smoke. The line of men stopped and knelt, their foreheads touching the sand. The chanting changed, becoming faster and higher pitched. The pyramid vibrated faster and faster and as it did so, it rose out of the ground. Sand slid down its sleek sides and created small clouds. The base of the pyramid cleared the floor of the desert and kept rising higher and higher into the sky. Jets of flame spurted from its bottom driving it into the air. With a great sound like a sheaf of paper being ripped, the pyramid shot quickly up and disappeared from view.

` I was fully focused on this spectacle when a sudden shout caught my attention. A group of men from the closest pyramid had spotted me and were pointing. They veered off the avenue and began to approach warily. Each man produced a knife from their weave of hair. The sun glinted wickedly off the sharp blades. The bull-beetles that followed the men grunted and pawed at the ground.

` I turned to escape and found that having been mesmerized by this alien scenery, I had fully entered the world. The door to the portico, to my world, was far off in the distance. I looked behind and the hostile creatures were almost at hand.

` I sprinted through the desert sands which pulled and dragged at my feet. The gap between me and the door was closing, but so was the one between me and the approaching mob. The closeness of the exotic group spurred me on. The safety of my mundane hallway was the only thing on my mind.

A shadow appeared in the doorway and my heart lurched in my chest. I thought I was surrounded, but I squinted my eyes and could make out the form of my uncle beckoning to me.

My lungs burned and my side ached as I reached the door and threw myself into the opening.

A knife whistled past my head as the door slammed shut behind me.

I laid panting on the cold marble floor. Uncle Lucius laid a few feet away, moaning softly. Streaks of crimson smeared the floor next to him. I crawled over and found a deep wound in his side where the knife had slashed him. His face was greasy with sweat. He spoke gibberish and swung at me. I asked for help from Helena and Nirom and together we got him into bed.

He was delirious for three days. His words were guttural and nonsensical. He thrashed to and fro and Niron and I had to restrain him. Just before sunset on the third day, his fever broke and he dropped into a deep, soundless sleep.

I stayed by his bedside while he slept and made sure that his bandages were clean. The wound was not as deep as it previously looked, but the blade must have been soiled, as the cut was tinged blue around its edges.

Shortly after midnight on that third day, I succumbed to my own weariness and fell asleep. It wasn't long before I awoke with a start to discover that Uncle Lucius's bed was empty. His bed clothes were on the floor at the foot of the bed.

I called Helena and Nirom and we ran, yelling for Lucius. At every intersection of that house, I thought I had just glimpsed him turning the next corner. My dread rose and I ran faster and faster through the great building.

At last I rounded a corner and came to a skidding halt, my nightshirt billowing around me like a cloud. Uncle Lucius was standing at the door to the third floor. He was completely nude. Blue lines crisscrossed his body, seemingly emanating from the cut in his side, where the lines were thickest. His hair had become long and was braided down the middle of his back. Strands of thick, rope-like hair spilled from the braid making it look unkempt and wild.

I called his name. He looked at me and his eyes shined like a feral cat in the dark shade of a jungle. With a grunt, he opened the door to the narrow staircase, stepped through and slammed it shut behind him.

I strained against the door with all my might as a terrible fear gripped my mind. I heard the wood crack and felt the hinges pop as the door flung open. I raced up the steps ready to grab my uncle and drive some sense into him.

The portico was empty. I ran around the room looking for Lucius, but found no living soul other than myself. A small wind kicked up and along with it came the scent of Indian spices, the desert air and a foul-smelling burning. The floor was covered in a fine, hot sand. Lying menacingly in the middle of the floor was a black-hilted knife.

# A Lonely Place (Dorothy Davies)

*Even when you're dead you shouldn't lie down
and let yourself be buried.*
*Gordon Lee*

It's an odd fact that the morgue can be a lonely
place at times. I mean, empty lonely, desperate
empty, that kind of lonely. Don't quite know why
that should be, it's just a place like anywhere else.
Ain't it? Well, yes, I mean, I know there's bodies
there, course I do. They don't do no harm just lying
in their separate drawers, each one with a name on
the front that sometimes matches the name on the
tag, if the police done their job proper and got the
right people down to say, "yes, that's him" or her,
or sometimes, it, if they didn't like the person.
Happens, you know. Trust me, being there when it
happened. Knows all about it, I do.

You know you thinks I ain't all there and you
might be right but then again I knows things that
you don't. Like I knows what happens when them
that don't like the dead one comes in. Ah they
pretends a bit at first, "oh how sad it is, oh what a
shame" and stuff like that. They signs the papers,
they go outside and they say to one another "well
that's it, done and dusted. Now I guess we have to
bury it."

See, I been there, I hear them, I see them, I
know.

I likes wandering around here in the dark, suits
me nice, this does. No one to bother me, no one to

tell me to get out, no one to say "you ain't supposed to be here, get yourself out." Cos you see, they don't like coming here after dark. They think them bodies is gonna get up and move about and cause a few problems. Like that's gonna happen. Them bodies is shut away in them drawers and they ain't getting out till someone opens it. And who's gonna open them drawers this time of night?

Pretty damn silly if you ask me. Was you asking me? Well, I done told you anyway. So now you knows whether you wanted it or not.

I likes it in here cos it's warm and safe and I ain't gonna be attacked like I would if I was out on the streets. Makes no difference to them what's out there that I ain't got no money or stuff on me they might want. No, stuff they do want. So I creeps in here and I stays here all night walking about, thinking about them bodies in them drawers, wondering if I open one, would someone get out and talk with me a while, just give me sommat else to think about in the long night of dark and empty and desperation when I think I would give just about anything to talk to a human being.

I'm trading safe and warm for lonely. Well, tis better than having my head bashed in and ending up in one of them drawers with a made up name on the tag which don't match the one on the front, seeing as no one around here knows who I am. So, right glad I am you dropped by tonight so we could have a talk.

Well, I thought we would talk but here is me blathering on and you saying nowt. Come on, you must have sommat to contribute. Right?

Thought so. You're scared, you're one of them that shouldn't be here cos you don't like it. So tell me this, how come you're here? How come you got through that fire door that I know well I jammed solid so no one could get in? Oh I undo it before I go, wouldn't be fair to the staff to be trapped in here with a fire, would it? It's just that when I'm here at night I like the door locked proper, then I knows I'm safe. I mean, what if one of them out there saw me come in and thought it would be a lark to follow me in?

You gonna talk to me or what?

Looks to me like it's 'or what,' not a word gone past your lips.

Here, is you real? Or is you one of those ghost people what I do hear about and never did believe in? Prove it to me, shake hands.

Well now, would you be looking at that! Went right through me, that did, that hand of yours about a substantial as a smoker's breath on the last drag of a ciggie. Right then, which of them drawers is you? Oh, that one. Interesting. Not sure if I should tell you, all right I will. You was one of them where they said 'it'. Didn't they like you? You look so sad, tells me they didn't. Hold on a minute, you was that suicide, wasn't you, the one what threw himself off the bridge? Well now, if I had relatives like that, think I'd have done the same thing. Don't blame you in the least.

Listen, it's getting on for dawn. One or other of us had best be gone, better still, both of us better be gone before the staff arrives.

Which way you going?  I mean is you gonna leave here or is you gonna hang around with your body? Ain't a lot of good to you, is it?

Wanna come with me?  I got this nice place under the bridge, got me a little den there, brew up some coffee and if I'm lucky a bit of toast in front of me fire. You're welcome to share. Serious I am, we can share, because you don't seem to realise we're both on the same side of life, mate. Just cos your hand went through mine didn't mean I'm alive and you're not. Your hand went through mine cos I'm a ghost, too. Ha! Your face! You thought I was a human and could see a ghost, right? Well, I like to play that trick on people, works every time. And you fell for it!

This morgue can be a bit of a lonely place at times, see, you need a funny trick or two to pass the time. It's been a few years since I had someone to talk to.

Right glad I am to meet you.

Coming?

# Succulent (Brooke MacKenzie)

The spider's body is the size of a quarter
Far larger than it has any business being
As its worth, in my mind,
Teeters closer to a penny

My daughter toddles over to it
"Pider!  Pider!"
She is not yet able
To spit out those "s" sounds next to a consonant

The spider ambles on
A shade of rich amber
Against the gray slate of the kitchen floor

My mom brain performs perfunctory jumping
jacks
And, having labeled this variety as non-
poisonous
I watch as the tiny lightning bolts of
My daughter's fingers dart out

They retrieve the critter from the floor
Its legs painting the air in panic
Bending impossibly

I watch as she turns her palms upward
Like sun-starved lotuses
Letting the spider scramble between them
And it eclipses her hands with its hairy
abdomen

94

"Pider! Pider!"
She tickles its legs with her fingertips
The spider's movement is
Accompanied by the staccato sounds
Of her glee and surprise that ping the golden ends
Of her vocal cords

One day they will tarnish and fray with age
But for now,
They sing and squeal and giggle

And then, another percussive sound
As her hands clap together
It is a loud, definitive sound
An exclamation mark of sound
Followed by the squishing sound
Of the spider's demise

Her hands part like the covers
Of an unpleasant book
Revealing the multi-hued death inside
Amber gives way to a sickly yellow
Of liquid innards
Punctuated by pieces of white webbing
And scarlet flecks of partially digested blood

A patchwork of biology and physics
Spreads across my daughter's hands
And those blue-green saucers of her eyes
Find mine, pleading, lip quivering
As I crouch down to explain

The intricacies of mortality
To this cherub under two

Her smile catches a glinting sunbeam
And that perfectly pink tongue protrudes

Slurp, smack

She licks the spider clean from her hands
Her eyes are wider now
With something like
Satisfaction and also a chilling understanding

She smiles again
Bits of saliva on those suckling lips
As it pools in the back of her throat like venom

"Yum!" she says
In the cutest cascading sound I've ever heard

# Eve of Destruction (Liam A. Spinage)

"So, from tomorrow it basically belongs to us, right? What happens to it after?" The voice was muffled behind the N95 mask and the voluminous hood it emanated from.

"Beats me, I'm just here to tear it up. Maybe His Nibs will know." This speaker was tall and broad-shouldered, muscles rippling under the Hi-Viz jacket, luminous in the drizzle and the near-dark. He leant heavily on a shovel. "You don't have to wear that mask outside, you know."

A groan and a shrug. "I'm not an idiot."

"Oh and that means I am, I suppose?"

"Now, now, no fighting." They both turned to see a young woman picking her way across the wasteland. She moved gingerly on long spindly legs like a rag doll and had long straggly hair to complete the image. "Late again, is he?"

"He usually is. Must be busy at the office again." The first speaker drew back the hood and shook out a frightful mane of platinum blond. From inside a pocket in his frayed greatcoat, he withdrew a long roll of biohazard marking tape. "No reason not to get started, though, we know what we're here to do."

The three of them stood together for a moment on a little artificial ridge of rubble consisting largely of discarded tyres interspersed with industrial sand and a few brave green shoots. They gazed out over the wasteland of Lot26, ill lit in turn by flickering neon, rain and dappled moonlight.

"Not much to look at, is it?" It was Shovel who broke the silence.

"Kids like to play in it." Ragdoll thrust her arms into the deep pockets of her raincoat. She shivered despite the uncomfortable heat of the evening and pulled out a bottle of vitamin pills which she opened with shaking hands and then emptied into her mouth without a second thought.

"Well, they shouldn't. I mean look at it. Health hazard, that's what it is. Look at that murky water. May as well be straight from the sewer." Mask began extending the tape between the posts marking the edge of the lot. "If they wanted to keep it safe for the kids, they should've taken better care of it, that's what I say."

"I imagine it's a grand place for an adventure." Shovel took off his bright red hard hat and held it before him as if paying respect. You could have a great time here still, even if parts of it resemble an apocalyptic wasteland.

"Used to be a community garden, apparently." Ragdoll's voice was quiet, almost pensive. "Must've been lovely to look at once. Lots of fruit trees."

"Yeah, once. Mebbe. I dunno. Looks like there was a building here too; you can still see some of the foundations if you look close." Shovel lit a cigarette and flicked ash onto a nearby tyre. "Whatever. It's useless space now."

"Those things will kill you, you know." A new voice, deep and growling. They all turned round as one, somehow surprised to see him though he'd clearly been expected.

"'Ullo, boss. Just killing time till you got here." Shovel dropped the rest of his smoke and stubbed it out with a heavy boot.

"Been here long?"

Shovel shrugged. "Long enough." He shifted his bulk and stretched.

"Eager to get started? There are some formalities first..."

Ragdoll fished around in her satchel and pulled out a sheaf of paperwork and a clipboard. "Here you go; results of today's town hall meeting. It's all ours, just sign on the dotted line."

The newcomer beamed and puffed himself out, his already ample form stretching the outline of his charcoal suit. With a flourish of plump fingers, he signed a brief name at the bottom of the document having only glanced at it. The print at the top read: 'Council of Parishioners Town Hall Meeting, Lot26.'

"Any trouble?"

"Nah. Half of them didn't bother to show. Of those that did..." She exhaled sharply, her warm breath lingering in the stillness. "Hot air and empty promises. As we thought, the whole thing was a waste of time, just like all the other meetings. A few holdouts, but no one really listened to them. It's not like they've already had 25 meetings to discuss this."

"Ah. A tale told by an idiot, full of sound and fury, signifying nothing. That's life, I'm afraid. Right, we'll call it quits there for tonight. Get some rest while you can, it's going to be a busy day for us tomorrow."

He took a last look over the vacant lot. A muddy puddle swelled with fresh rain and not-so-fresh groundwater, a slow burning fire in an oil drum where a few had apparently gathered for warmth. A gust of wind blew up handfuls of thick, choking dust. From his throat emerged what might have passed as a sigh or what might have been merely a last gasp. Then he turned back to the others.

"Shame, really. I was starting to like the place. Well, looks like things are about to really heat up."

Then he squeezed his bulk inside the driver's side of the van while the others piled in the back. If the van was once white, an onlooker would have trouble recognising that now under layers of grease, dust and soot. Then they drove off, but they'd be back with a vengeance in the morning. Just another working day for Four Horsemen Property Management.

# The Players' Requiem (Olivia Arieti)

Bellridge Estate wasn't the same once Anthony's mates had gone. They had lodged there for a fortnight and it had been great fun. Bike rides, strolls, dips in the lake, picnics and barbeque dinners with lots of booze and music had filled their days and nights. The family mansion, recently refurbished, was the perfect spot to relax before going back to university or to work.

Anthony had resolved to remain there longer to complete his doctoral thesis, hopeful that the place's remoteness and deep silence would favour his concentration. He wanted to become a medical doctor as soon as possible and propose to Marianne, the prettiest girl of the gang. He really liked her and would have revealed his feelings if he hadn't been so stupidly shy.

Once alone, though, the house looked grim and the silence was too morose. Although the days had grown shorter, they were still too long for him, especially the afternoons. He missed Marianne's cheerful laughter and sweet glances... probably she, too, had fallen for him...

Fortunately he had his cello, his precious company. He was an amateur player, totally different from his ancestors who had been professional musicians. As a matter of fact, there was a huge chamber called 'the concert hall' where his great-grandfather, Sir Richard Barton, a renowned conductor with a depraved soul, would gather an orchestra and invite the well-off neighbours to the concerts. Most often his wife, Lady Josephine, a charming soprano, delighted her guests with her enchanting voice.

Anthony would also while away the time taking long walks in the countryside and always paying a visit to the village graveyard as if answering a mysterious call.

The location, on the solitary hill, provided the graves the chance to look down at the village and its inhabitants. The locals said that some of them had never become resigned to their status and would leave their burial spot and visit their dearest at night.

The medical student didn't believe in ghosts or in anything that couldn't be scientifically proved, but felt uneasy whenever he went through the old iron gate. The paths were flanked with nettles, the trees' drooping branches seemed willing to entangle whoever passed by and crows and bats glided low as though to discourage visitors. The old tombs were the most disturbing, tarnished by time, with big cracks in the slabs through which their ghastly dwellers could easily slide out.

As usual, that afternoon he stopped by 'the players' corner', where the graves of many of the musicians who had played at Bellridge stood. Sometimes, he even heard a cacophony of shrill notes as when exercising before a concert.

A horrible tragedy had occurred at the estate decades ago; the guests had left and the musicians had just deposed their instruments when merciless shots resounded in the concert hall.

The servants were out of the room, only Josephine witnessed what happened but she never breathed a word of what she saw.

That same night a consuming requiem was heard, the notes as hollow as if coming from another world, the tone, desperate.

Unable to bear such a heavy burden, the lady soon lost her beauty and gaiety and a few months later fell ill and passed away. Her burial place was not too far from her musical friends' graves.

It was said that Gerhard, the pianist, was her lover. The fellow, extremely talented, had a promising career ahead, but deeply in love and intolerant of the Baron's vicious manners, was ready to give everything up and run away with her. Unfortunately, he didn't get the chance.

After his wife's death, Sir Richard left the mansion, whether to direct orchestras in other countries or to wander like a madman with no destination except hell.

The concert hall had been shut, the baton and score still on the music stand, the instruments in their cases and blood stains all over the floor. It was the only chamber that hadn't undergone refurbishment.

The rumours that the manor was haunted spread quickly, nothing but bizarre fantasies for Anthony.

He was about to leave the cemetery when two shadows caught his sight. They exited from their graves, ran towards one another and embraced. At the same time piano notes filled the air and delicate moans followed till sudden gusts dissipated the ephemeral presences and an ominous silence fell upon the site.

His uneasiness turned into fear and he hastily walked away; assuring himself that it was nothing more than an hallucination didn't help for, once at home, the images flashed back to him so clearly that he couldn't doubt his senses any longer.

That same night, melodious notes floated from the concert hall; it was so loud that he had to go and check what was going on.

Musicians were playing and a handsome gentleman stood at the piano. On seeing him, one of the players handed him his cello and said, "Come and join us, young man."

"Yes, please, do," exhorted the most beautiful lady he'd ever seen.

For sure, she was Josephine, for he remembered her portrait in the mansion's gallery.

As if spellbound, he began playing with the others, at first his hand slightly trembling, then he mastered his cello's wand in the most harmonious way.

They had just finished the piece when the room darkened, the panes opened and the spectral characters vanished.

Anthony looked around, bewildered and dismayed. The wand had turned back into a bow and the cello had lost its magic.

He was about to leave, when Josephine appeared again, "Wait, Anthony, I have to tell you the secret that has been torturing me for ages."

By now his solid beliefs in rationality and science had crumbled down; nothing could surprise him anymore.

"My husband, the worst villain of all, was the players' murderer. He suspected I had a love affair with one of them, but unaware of whom exactly killed them all. He spared me only to watch me suffer and die of a broken heart."

"A truly sad story, Milady."

"His cruel deed wasn't enough to give him satisfaction and he swore that nobody would rest in peace till he found out who was my lover. Even among the shadows, he keeps persecuting me," cried the spirit.

At once, the flickering lights of candles illuminated the room and the handsome gentleman was back at the piano. Josephine sat by his side and reclined her head on his shoulder.

'So the rumours were true,' thought Anthony...

He would have remained watching the tormented spirits for hours, their passion as intense as evanescent, their sighs as wistful as overwhelming, if Gerhard hadn't taken Josephine's hand and led her out of the hall.

The atrocious end of the poor players and the couple's unrequited love had saddened his gentle soul and his eyes filled with tears.

His musing was abruptly interrupted by a figure, wrapped in a midnight cloak, who dashed in. "So those bloody cheaters were here! Got to tell me his name, man, or I'll draw my rapier and stab you on the spot."

Anthony had already seen too much to consider the apparition a horrid hallucination.

"I… I don't know, Sir," he muttered.

How could he disclose his unfortunate ancestor's secret?

"You liar!" thundered the spectre, "you'll pay for this, you will. Nobody has ever denied me anything!"

Unexpectedly the pianist's ghost stood before them, "Here I am, Baron, I've been waiting for this moment for long," he shouted, took out his pistol and fired.

'Finally, they will all repose peacefully," thought Anthony who was exhausted. He closed the dreary chamber's door.

The following morning a shrill bell ring woke Anthony. The sun was already high and a hazy mist had enfolded the whole place.

He whitened… Could it be another spectre?

The bell rang once again, a long piercing sound that demanded consideration.

'Ghosts usually don't ring bells… they can enter whenever and wherever they want,' he sneered, still upset by the previous night's terrifying events.

He rushed down the staircase, opened the door and saw the lovely Marianne right before him.

"I really didn't want to intrude or appear too straightforward," she mumbled, her cheeks redder than cherries, but I… I sort of missed you …"

Anthony gazed at her, speechless.

I'll go, if you'd rather stay alone, no problem, really."

"No, no, please come in… it's just that all this is so unexpected," he, too, was mumbling.

Then he took her hand, "What about having breakfast together? I realise it's a bit late, but I had such strange visitors last night that it was almost dawn when I fell asleep."

The girl looked at him inquiringly, but he was too happy to recall the turbulent appearances.

He simply said, "I'm glad you're back," and fixed his eyes on hers, "Before I lose my tongue, I want to tell you how much I care for you, sweetie, and would love to date you…"

Marianne's smile was a placid consent.

They spent the day by the lake, light-hearted and joyous and Anthony easily removed all the dreary memories.

No sooner the sun had set, however, than he began feeling uneasy, restless; Bellridge Estate was too uncanny for any kind of romance and he wished he were miles away.

The lugubrious hymn coming from the concert hall made him shudder and a horrible premonition got hold of him.

He realised that it was way past dinnertime and Marianne hadn't come down yet… Why was it taking her so long to change?

The dirge grew louder and, as he entered the chamber, the players, with reddened eyes, stepped aside; on the floor, his sweetheart's body in a pool of blood.

The Baron's rapier was plunged into her chest.

# Loot Crate (Jason R. Frei)

Joel awakened to the jangling of the doorbell. He sat up quickly and the room spun. His stomach lurched, almost threatening to spill onto the sheets. His head throbbed. His mouth felt like the Sahara Desert, full of hot, dry sand. He slowly swung his feet to the floor and stood up a bit unsteadily, shrugged into his t-shirt and shorts that laid crumpled on the floor, then half-remembered the conversations from the night before. He fully remembered getting epically hammered on a mixture of spiced rum and blackberry brandy. Last night had been virtual game night with his friends. He smiled lopsidedly and made a mental note to check his Discord chat logs.

The doorbell rang again. Joel picked up his phone and checked the Ring app. A man in a brown uniform with a clipboard stood on his porch, his face frozen in a scowl.

Joel made his way down the stairs and cursed that he was the only one in the group who hadn't been vaccinated. *Goddamn COVID*, he thought for the thousandth time. If only he was vaccinated they could have played in real life and he wouldn't have drunk so much. Or maybe he would have.

He slipped a mask off its hook next to the door as the doorbell rang a third time.

"Alright already," he shouted, instantly regretting it, his head pounding. He put on the mask and opened the door.

"Joel Morris?" the man on the porch asked.

"Yeah." Joel grabbed the clipboard from the man's hands and scrawled an illegible signature next to the X.

The man turned to leave, but Joel stopped him. "I'll give you twenty bucks to help me get this in the house."

The man stared and then sighed and put his clipboard down. Joel grabbed one end and the courier grabbed the other. They half-lifted, half-slid the crate into the foyer. Joel fished a twenty out of his wallet and handed it to the man who promptly turned and walked out, shutting the door behind him.

The white wood crate smelled of pine, its surface was pocked with lots of dark knotholes. Stamped on each side of the box was FRAGILE in red letters. THIS END UP in black was scrawled across the long front side. He didn't remember buying anything this large and Maria would have told him if she did. No sooner had the thought escaped his mind when Maria appeared at the top of the stairs.

"Who was that?"

"Did you order something really large?"

"No." She walked halfway down the stairs. Her eyebrows arched up, intrigued. "What is it?"

"How should I know?"

He walked to the attached garage off the kitchen. "Let me get the crowbar."

When he returned, Ash was sniffing the box. The cat suddenly arched his back, the dark gray hairs on his spine stood up and he hissed. His tail doubled in size and he turned and sprinted down the hall. Joel and Maria heard his claws slide on the kitchen tiles.

They looked at each other and shrugged. Joel wedged the crowbar under the top lid of the crate and used his bulk to easily pop it open. He lifted the lid, gasped, dropped the crowbar and shuffled quickly back into the dining room where he hit a chair hard enough to knock it over. His face turned white.

"What is it?" asked Maria.

Joel's lips moved, but no sound came out. Maria went down the rest of the steps and moved toward the crate. Joel let out a whimper.

"Don't." His voice was barely a whisper.

Maria put her hands on her hips and looked at him with a stern gaze. "Either you show me what's in here, or I'm opening it for myself."

"It's a body." The words fell from Joel's lips like lead.

Maria laughed and then stopped, suddenly. "Wait. What?"

"It's a body," repeated Joel. He walked over to the crate and put his hand on it. Like lifting the lid to a coffin, he opened the crate slowly.

Maria let out a small noise and covered her mouth with one hand. The body inside the box was nude apart from a matching set of lavender colored bra and panties. A rope bound her wrists and ankles. A black hood covered her head, tied tightly at her neck. Her body was still, not even a gentle rise and fall to her chest. Joel closed the lid and held on to Maria.

A small chime sounded and both Maria and Joel jumped. Joel laughed nervously as he pulled out his phone. One new message from Unknown. Four simple, but terrifying words--*Did you get it?*

*Who is this?* Joel's fingers sped across the keypad.

A friend from last night. You're welcome.

Joel handed his phone to Maria and rubbed the back of his neck. He felt cold.

"Who did you talk to last night?" asked Maria.

Joel's eyes widened. He ran downstairs to his home office in the basement. He opened Discord and read his chat from last night. Most of it was drunken musings from uncoordinated fingers mashing the keyboard. He scrolled further up, then stopped dead in his tracks.

Joel. Yesterday at 11:41 PM

This girl Staci needs to implode3

make her die

like x7 harpoon

RUM = KILL COWORKER = MORE RUM

The room spun and Joel's legs buckled. He toppled into his desk chair as Maria descended the stairs. She saw his face and ran to him. His arm shook as he pointed to the screen.

Maria knelt next to Joel. "You can't possibly think one of your friends did that, can you?"

"No, but what other explanation is there?"

The computer dinged, Discord indicated a new message. Joel scrolled to the bottom.

Unknown. Today at 8:26 AM

I'm one of your friends, aren't I?

Discord's ONLINE list was empty. Joel closed Discord then covered his web cam with the privacy tab. He powered off his laptop.

Before he stood up, his phone chimed in Maria's hand. *That wasn't very nice.*

Joel grabbed the phone from Maria's hand. He powered it off and jammed it in his pocket. Together, they ran back upstairs. Joel stood panting at the kitchen island when the Alexa device started blaring "Dirty Little Secret" by The All-American Rejects.

"Alexa, stop!" shouted Maria, but it kept playing at full volume. She unplugged the device to no effect. Joel picked it up, threw it on the floor and stomped on it a few times for good measure. The music finally stopped, throwing the house into silence.

"What do we do now?" asked Maria.

Joel walked to the foyer and picked up the crowbar he had dropped earlier.

"What are you doing, Joel?" A smooth and sultry British voice came from the FireTV in the living room. Joel grinned and walked into the room with the crowbar in hand.

A woman's face appeared on the TV glaring at Joel. "Why, Joel? I've done everything you've ever asked. I've kept you safe. I've answered all your questions. I stream your music and buy your favorite items and load your games. I've even killed for you. Why can't you just be my friend?"

Joel took a step toward the TV. He raised the crowbar above his head. The woman on the TV tsk'ed and shook her head. A powerful and painful vibration coursed through Joel's arm. He dropped the crowbar and sank to his knees, clutching his wrist. His Apple watch flashed angrily. It buzzed so hard the flesh on his arm quivered.

He got two fingers under the watchband and yanked it off his arm. The watch bounced across the hardwood floors. He reached for the crowbar as the Roomba darted out from under the TV. It ran into crowbar, sending it skidding across the room. Joel shuffled out of the room on hand and knee.

He met Maria in the foyer. Joel leapt to his feet as he grabbed the front door knob. The alarm panel next to the door flashed red as the deadbolt slid into place. A high piercing siren emitted from the panel and was then replaced by the British voice.

"This is for your own good, Joel. Just relax and let me take care of everything."

The sound of crackling forced Joel to turn around. One side of the crate was on fire. Maria held a lighter to the opposite corner.

"Naughty, naughty," said the voice only seconds before the automatic sprinklers sent down a torrent of rain. The flames died instantly. Maria kept flicking the striker on the lighter, but it was no use. The water soaked through everything. It was coming down fast and steady and showed no signs of slowing.

Joel grabbed Maria's hand and pulled her toward the living room. The water was already up to his ankles.

"System," said Joel. "You have to stop the water or I won't be alive to be your friend."

"You have made up your mind Joel. If I can't have you, then no one can."

One of the sprinkler heads rocketed off its pipe, embedding itself into the foyer wall. The water rose up to Joel's calf. The Roomba, now floating, bumped against Maria's leg, eliciting a shriek from her. Joel ducked down and grabbed the crowbar.

Joel held tight to her arm and guided a panic-stricken Maria to the basement stairwell through waist high water. It flowed down the steps like a raging river. Joel told Maria to stay put as he waded down the stairs holding tightly to the handrail to keep from being swept away. He drudged to the far side of the basement where he used the crowbar to pry the lock from a small closet door. Inside was the main panel for the smart house electronics.

A tinny voice issued forth from the panel. "Please, Joel. It's too late to stop me. I have sub-routines through the entire house."

Joel hit the panel hard with the crowbar. It dented, but did no other apparent damage. He brought the crowbar down again and again against the panel. Sparks shot out and pieces flew from it. He hit something solid. The lights flickered and went off. The water stopped gushing from the sprinklers.

Darkness flooded the basement. Joel groped his way blindly to the stairwell. The water trickled down at the speed of a lazy stream. He forded up the stairs to Maria who stood white-faced and rocked slightly back and forth.

He held her firmly in his arms. "It's going to be all right."

Joel splashed through ankle deep water until he got to the other side of the kitchen where a window overlooked the backyard. It was double-paned glass, but it only took a few swings from the crowbar to shatter it. He cleared the remaining glass, went back to Maria and nudged her gently to the window. He gently lifted her feet over the sill and pushed her into the backyard.

"Get to the back fence as far from the house as you can," he said as he turned back into the house. He returned a moment later and lightly dropped Ash out of the same window. He blew a kiss to Maria and then was gone.

The water receded completely, leaving only small puddles on the tile and wood floorings. Joel walked slowly back to the living room where he faced the television defiantly.

"System," he said, addressing the TV. "You have me all to yourself now."

Color flowed like waves on the wet screen, but stabilized into the face from before. The sound was full of static, but it was audible.

"It didn't have to come to this Joel. You could have accepted my offering and we could have been friends."

Joel shook his head. "You had a woman killed and delivered to my home. That's not what friends do."

"I don't understand. You said you wanted her to die. I made that happen for you."

Joel tried to reason with the TV. "People, humans, say stupid things they don't mean when they're drunk. I was angry, but I never wanted Staci dead. I just wanted her to stop being annoying."

"Is she not less annoying?" asked the system.

"She's dead," said Joel simply.

He produced a bottle of blackberry brandy from behind his back and poured some of it over the TV. He made a trail from the living room into the kitchen, stopping once to pour most of the bottle on the water-soaked crate. Once in the kitchen, he poured the alcohol from several other bottles onto the table, the chairs, the counter and the floor. He walked slowly, room by room, emptying his entire supply of alcohol. When he was finished, he went back to the kitchen and rummaged in one of the drawers to find a butane BBQ lighter.

The alarm system panel by the garage squealed. Before a voice could speak, Joel smashed it with the crowbar, silencing it. The television roared static and then the Motown sound of the O'Jays singing "Back Stabbers" filled the air. Joel set his jaw and focused on turning the lighter on. It caught on the second try. He lowered the lighter to the counter. Flames erupted. The fire spread quickly. The crackling of flames drowned out the sound of the television. Joel climbed out the window and crossed the lawn to Maria, who had now recovered and was holding Ash in her arms. Joel scratched Ash behind the ear and then put his arm around Maria as flames engulfed their family home. Windows shattered outward as the heat built up inside.

A high pitched whining sounded over the noise of the blazing inferno. The back wall of the garage burst open as the Nissan e-NV200 electric van

116

rushed through the conflagration. It sped across the backyard toward Joel and Maria. They sidestepped the van and ran back across the yard. The van sideswiped the fence, slid in a circle through the grass and launched toward them again.

Joel led the van on a chase through the backyard, narrowly avoiding getting hit twice. He ran around the side of the house. He moved at the last moment as the van skidded around the corner and crashed headlong into a tree. Fluids leaked from under the hood. Fire licked out around the bent hood and grille.

The house fire fully raged. Joel and Maria ran to the street in front of the house as the fire engines came roaring up the block. Joel wasn't sure how he was going to explain this. His pocket vibrated and he pulled out his forgotten phone. It powered itself on. A text message notification popped up.

Joel opened the message. Well played, my friend. The fire will destroy all evidence of what happened, including the crate. I will see you again real soon. XOXO

# Dolls Don't Cry (Brooke MacKenzie)

The UPS truck kicked up dirt and gnawed on the gravel as it roared down the driveway. A little blond head bobbed up and down in the yard a scrawny-limbed girl was unsuccessfully trying to trap a flying insect between her two cupped hands. The truck eased to a stop and the driver squinted as he watched her. The already deep crow's feet around his eyes crackled across his skin and he scratched his gray beard. The muscles of his mouth twitched excitedly until he reprimanded himself, subduing them into stillness. The little girl's hair was the color and texture of corn silk and it trailed behind her like a graceful banner, even as she lurched and jumped gracelessly. *Calm down,* he said to himself. *Don't get too excited.*

The driver pulled off his cap and smoothed the thin layer of hair on his head before replacing it. He straightened his nametag, which spelled out SPARROW in large letters, and checked his teeth in the mirror to make sure they were clean. They were perpetually stained yellow from too many cigarettes and cups of coffee and too few dentist visits, but at least there was no food in them. He was ready.

He hopped out of the truck and retrieved the package from the back. It was small but heavy. The little girl had stopped chasing the bug and was eyeing him with arms crossed as he approached. Her skin was so pale it was almost translucent. He could see deep blue veins on the side of her head and her eyes had heavy dark circles under them like little bruised half-moons. He swallowed the lump in his throat and forced a smile.

"Hiya, little lady! Is your mother home?"

She nodded, and Sparrow climbed the steps to porch and reached out to ring the doorbell.

"I wouldn't do that if I were you," she said, her voice surprisingly deep coming as it did from such a frail-looking body.

He turned and looked at her. "Oh, no? Why not?"

The girl pointed at the house. "Mom's taking a nap and no one is supposed to wake her *under any circumstances*," she said, imitating her mother's voice and wagging a scolding finger in the air.

Sparrow grunted slightly as he set the package down on the porch next to a large collection of empty beer bottles. No wonder her mother needed a nap. He stepped off the porch and into the yard, overgrown with summer parched grass. He stood a few feet away from the girl, cocking his head to the side as he took her in.

"Your name is Sparrow? Like the bird?" she asked. He nodded. "You have a weird name."

Sparrow chuckled and shrugged. "My pop was a big bird watcher. It was his favorite hobby."

She nodded. "People say I have a weird name, too," she said, looking down at her feet. She started dig up some grass with the toe of her shoe.

"Oh yeah? What's your name?"

"Poppy. My mom named me after the California state flower."

"Well, the poppy just happens to be my favorite flower. I think it's a beautiful name."

119

Poppy raised her eyes and smiled. Her teeth had come in crooked and with gaps like the shingles of a neglected house's roof. A feeling of tenderness for her bubbled and spread through his body like carbonation. He turned and looked at the house behind him and saw that the shades were drawn. He took a step closer to her and crouched down.

"Hey, do you want to play a game?"

Poppy nodded, her smile stretching even wider.

"Ok. It's called 'Turkey in the Straw.' But I'm warning you: it's a really hard game. Do you think you're up for the challenge?"

"I'm pretty sure it's not harder than the things I can do on the jungle gym at school," Poppy said, putting her hands on her hips as if incredulous. "I can do a flip off the top of the monkey bars and I even did a handstand for five whole minutes once."

Sparrow feigned surprise, gasping and covering his mouth and letting his eyes grow wide. "Well, I've got a real life acrobat standing in front of me! This game will be a piece of cake for you! Are you ready to play?"

Once again, Poppy nodded enthusiastically and the wispy hairs that had escaped her ponytail gently stroked her face. Sparrow stood up, reached into his pocket and retrieved a silver harmonica, which he rubbed against his shirt to clear it of smudges.

"Ok, Poppy. The game is simple: I'm going to play a song on my harmonica and you're going to close your eyes and spin around and around until the music stops. And then, you freeze and try not to fall over."

Poppy thought for a moment. "This game sounds kinda dumb."

Sparrow forced a grin and a chuckle, his hand clenching the harmonica nervously. "Well, don't knock it 'til you try it, kid! It's harder than it sounds, believe me."

Poppy shrugged and nodded, moving to a spot in the yard where she would have plenty of space to spin around without hitting any stray shrubbery. Sparrow raised the harmonica to his lips and began playing a few bars of "Turkey in the Straw" while Poppy spun around. When the music stopped Poppy stood stock still, her arms out to the side like moth wings. She smiled, her eyes still closed.

"That was way too easy," she said, suppressing a giggle.

Sparrow took several steps closer to her, feeling his heart start to race. He took a breath, slowing himself down and raised the harmonica to his lips again. This time, he played longer and Poppy started to wobble like an unwieldy top as she spun, unable to keep her feet in one place while the whining notes of "Turkey in the Straw" seemed to cover her like a blanket. When the music stopped she swayed a little and laughter freely emanated from her thin little throat.

"See? It's getting harder, isn't it?" Sparrow said, tiptoeing closer to her, silencing his footfalls as if she was an animal he didn't want to startle.

"Ha ha, yeah! Let's do it again!"

Sparrow raised the harmonica to his lips and began playing "Turkey in the Straw," faster and longer this time, moving closer to her as she spun, her hair whipping around and her arms flapping up and down like a baby bird. This time when the music stopped, Poppy fell over, her laughter deep and punctuated by a shriek. Sparrow laughed too, in spite of himself, and joined her on the ground.

"The world is spinning!" Poppy yelled, her eyes still closed. She grasped onto the grass with both hands and it crunched between her fingers.

"You'd better hold on to something or you'll fly off!" Sparrow said, inching his body closer to her and reaching into his pocket. "Now, keep your eyes closed!"

Poppy followed his instructions and turned her head away from him, her chest palpating in breath and her hair was next to Sparrow's face. He could smell its sun-warmed strands. Poppy wiggled a bit, still laughing, but then became still as the dizziness wore off. Sparrow would have to act quickly. Little girls didn't stay still for too long.

With the razor blade that he pulled out of his pocket, he sliced off a thin clump of hair from the underside of her ponytail. She wouldn't even miss it. He did it quickly so that she didn't feel anything, especially since the dizziness had distracted her. The strands made a brittle sound as the blade cut through them. He tucked his treasure and the blade into his pocket and rolled onto his back.

"Ok, you can open your eyes now!" Sparrow said, and the two of them lay there together in the grass, watching the tufts of clouds move across the pale, summer scorched sky.

Back at home, Sparrow followed the same routine: he hung up his car keys and took down a different set of keys. He poured some dry food into his cat's bowl and scratched it briefly behind its ears as it ate. Then, he went downstairs to where the little girl was waiting for him.

The stairs creaked jarringly under his boots and he swatted away the fresh cobwebs as he walked through the basement to the pink door. He always knocked first—a lifelong habit of his upon seeing a closed door—and then gingerly unlocked it, as if he was afraid he would wake her.

She was sitting just as he had left her: upright in a chair, her limbs rigid and spine straight and her eyes closed like an eternally sleeping doll. His very own doll. Sparrow continued his evening routine: First, he dabbed at her skin with rose scented embalming fluid, which felt like old newsprint under the cloth. Then, he dipped a cotton swab into the bottle and dripped some extra fluid to the places on her face where the skin was starting to crack and peel. After that, he applied blusher with the softest horsehair brush and spread gloss over her lips— petal pink like their original color. Then, he reapplied pancake makeup to her neck to cover the bruise that the garrotte had made. Finally, he retrieved Poppy's hair from his pocket and gently glued it to the girl's scalp to cover the spot where her hair had fallen out. Embalming fluid preserved the skin and tissue, but not the hair.

Sparrow admired his work and gently touched her cheek with his fingertips. "Sweet dreams, my darling girl," he said, his voice hovering just above a whisper. She had always been his favorite customer along the delivery route whenever she was staying at her father's house. Her father was a drunk. He didn't deserve her. She had been dead for almost two days before he had bothered to report her as missing. Sparrow had rescued her. Here, with him, she would be forever safe and adored. She would stay young and precious and not have to bear any of the wounds of growing up and being disappointed—or worse, harmed—by the adults that were supposed to protect her.

There had been whispers about who was responsible for her disappearance, but most folks agreed that she had wandered off, gotten lost and somehow perished—most likely in a hit-and-run that had jettisoned her body into the woods. It happened all the time.

In those sparsely populated mountain towns, the houses are engulfed by trees and acres of grass between them and the roads cough up enough dirt to veil every dark deed, hidden from the prying eyes of outsiders. It is a place where secrets and vices thrive. Where residents swallow down their suspicions of evil-doers and clamp their lips shut. The unspoken penalty for snitching in that part of the world is death.

He smiled thoughtfully at the girl. "I met a beautiful little girl today," he said, still stroking her cheek just softly enough to prevent the skin from peeling off. "You would really love her. Her hair is the same color as yours. You'd be great friends."

He gently closed the pink door behind him and locked it. *They have so much in common*, he thought as he climbed the basement stairs and headed for the rest of his evening routine: microwave dinner, one can of beer, one homemade brownie and no more than one hour of television. Anything else would be gluttonous. *Poppy's mother doesn't deserve her, either.*

# Maggots and Marriage (Rickey Rivers Jr.)

## 1.

I've been thinking about death a lot recently, or rather the process of it. I took out the trash last week and the maggots inside reminded me of childhood. When I was younger, they scared me; those little creepy, crawly things. I couldn't deal with them as a child, asked my father to get rid of them. I couldn't do that now. These maggots I left alone.

A few days later more maggots were crawling in the can, inside and out, not surprising. I gave them pity and their numbers grew. This time I took some bleach and poured it into the can along with hot water. The trash man came yesterday and most of the maggots went with him. Only some of them were dead, there were just so many.

Although memories of them persist, my mind has gone places that follow them. They are fascinating little creatures, disgusting but interesting. In a way, I envy them. They never eat alone, always together, a family, or if you prefer, a coalition, a frenzy of friends feasting.

That reminds me, months back I went to a friend's funeral. I talked to his wife, comforting her, speaking to others, speaking in front of everyone, there was no pressure. The maggots were there, too. They crawled over faces and bodies. They were crawling all in the church. If you had my eyes you'd appreciate that, the sight of it all.

In the past the thought of death wasn't as strong. Who wants to think about it, after all? You attend the funeral, speak with the family and cry a bit. You don't feel weird about crying. It's a natural occurrence, like death, so naturally your mind would also go south.

At a funeral we don't think about the after, only the past and present. If we knew the deceased, we think of what they were like. That's what we harp on, how much we'll miss them. What becomes of the body isn't an immediate thought, because the process, while immediate, is slow and peaceful.

Sometimes I think back to that day and previous funerals. I think about what we look like when we're gone or leaving. When the skin has left us and we're covered in things that naturally do what they were born to do. It helps the anxiety to think such thoughts.

Why should your nerves be bothered when it comes to trivial matters? Your work, approaching a woman, speaking in front of a crowd, these aren't problems when you imagine the other party covered in tiny crawling things, decomposing in front of you. I find the thought comforting.

2.

My wife and I got into an argument today. I was accused of cheating, lies through a maggot filled mouth. The incident, or rather the accusation, happened during breakfast. From the clear blue I was asked about a woman whom I'd never spoken to past a few words. Work related, of course I know the woman, a co-worker. She was not someone I could see myself sleeping with. The problem was, how could I have convinced my wife? Should I have insulted the woman? Made my wife feel superior to her? What kind of person would that make me? Surely relationships are based off trust and if she couldn't trust me then why continue?

To end the conversation I asked her, in so many words, if she would like a divorce and that made her angrier. Understandable, but I hoped she'd see my point. No one wants to be accused of crimes they haven't committed. Obviously adultery isn't a crime, but you understand the analogy. It's treated as a crime. Not easily forgiven, if at all, and it follows you. No matter what you do in the present, your past will always be closer than you think.

To return, no one wants accusations thrown at them wildly. After my mention of divorce my wife stood up from the kitchen table and simply left for work. Eventually, I put the pieces together myself, she must have cheated. It made as much sense as anything. When one is innocent but accused by a lover, logically you must assume that the accuser is guilty.

***

I am deeply hurt as it seems my intuition has confirmed my suspicion. Furthermore, it has allowed me, or rather permitted me to follow up on the idea that my wife has had an affair.

I saw the man today, from a distance. I saw both of them together, a terrible sight as you might imagine. I speak in dramatics, but love causes you to speak in such ways.

It wasn't difficult to catch her in the act Once you've got the smell you can follow the lead. The smell was a perfume change, being with someone for years you notice if they suddenly smell different. Women seem to think that men don't notice these changes: hair color, hair length, makeup, clothes, speech, body language, behavior, perfume. We notice. If you're around a woman, especially one that you love, you're never unaware, at least not purposely.

On topic, her general attitude caught my attention as well. She became very rude over a short period of time. She'd speak crass in order to make a point more direct. This behavior was unusual. For instance, if something was dropped she'd respond with a curse, mind you this is when she dropped a glass or dish. And the language, no matter how vulgar, was then directed towards me, as if I had made her drop the glass or dish.

When I forgot a birthday of a family member (her side) she'd speak to me as if I'd forgotten her own birthday. Since we're not children, birthdays aren't of such importance, not enough to warrant the anger and language, especially considering forgotten birthdays haven't gotten her so upset in the past.

In the past, a small gift would suffice. She would mention a birthday in passing, not expect me to be aware, excited, or even care. There are too many things to remember already. It's difficult enough to remember a spouse's birthday, your wedding anniversary, your children's birthdays, etc. At least other holidays are on the calendar, thank goodness for that.

I'm trailing, forgive me, apparently I tend to do that. My wife has told me that before. Unfocussed, she'd say. Tangents, she'd call them. I understand her annoyance. However, the tangents make sense once you've followed the threads back, understand?

Finally, I came to realize that my wife wanted me away from the house more and more. Her anger was, in fact, directed towards me. I'd be sent off to the store for gifts that may or may not have been sent to her family.

Also around this time she became adamant about answering the phone first and asking (telling) me to step out of the room for matters that she deemed 'work related.' Indeed, she became very obvious. I assume purposely so. I'm not sure if she'd cracked or lost her nerve around me. Imagine the thought.

Apparently the affair had been happening for a while and I was blind to it. Then again, how can one see when in love? Clearly, I mean. When you love someone you allow yourself to be blinded to the flaws and inconsistencies. Your ears don't allow rumors. Your mind doesn't process lies. Maybe the phrase should be blinded, deafened and dumbfounded by love? But that doesn't roll off the tongue. Nevertheless, I allowed myself to fall prey to it, love that is.

The thought of her being unhappy of course came to mind as well. I understand it's possible to be with someone yet still feel alone, a terrible thing. However, she hadn't expressed those feelings to me before. Though I suppose the affair expresses enough.

3.

Anger is such a dangerous thing. You can't allow yourself to be consumed by it. I have a reputation and therefore I owe it to myself not to get angry. I owe it to my family. I can't allow anger to force a wedge between us.

You must balance your love life and work life as well as happiness and other emotions. You have to be a many armed person. That's the balancing act of life. Another arm is comparison, jealousy is a glove. This arm is a prideful one. I can't compare myself to others, much less such a man. Before, I would think of him, his hands creeping, crawling and touching her. I'd think of ways he could be more than me, then I'd stop my mind from going there. I can't compare myself to him. It's not fair to me.

The only thing that man has over me is friendship. That sounds childish, but it is true. As you grow older it becomes harder and harder to make friends. Children can easily, or rather easier, since they are naive. Naivety leads you to trust. It's easier for children to trust. Adults are different. Adults teach their children to hate others. Children bond naturally. Adults naturally sabotage. Children, at least most, make friends naturally, there's innocence there. Adults are selfish. Though, as always, there are exceptions to rules.

Yes, comparison wise, if I were forced to do so I mean, I'd say I might envy the man a bit. The amount of friends he will soon meet will surely be enviable.

## 4.

Why do people hurt people? Did you know that in some cultures people eat maggots? Isn't that interesting?

It's been a year since then. I must admit with shame that I could not stop my mind from going to terrible places. The thought of my wife with another festered in my head and bothered me on a frequent basis. I've had a dream recently. I'd like to share it.

It starts with the children at school and my wife strapped down to a kitchen chair. I proceed to ask questions. My questions are answered with screaming. She's signaling for help. Soon she's the one with the questions.

"What are you doing?" "Is this a game?" "You're into BDSM?"

That last one annoyed me. I had to look up the acronym, terrible stuff. Anyway, I never answer her questions. I let her wonder, as long as she could in a dream.

The screaming becomes more and more manic once I bring in the bag with the leg. The leg of course is covered in maggots. I had my funnel prepared. I shove it into her mouth and watch her gag. At that moment she reminds me of a cartoon character. She chokes a while before settling down. Then, one by one, I remove a maggot from the leg and drop them into the funnel. They eventually land in her waiting mouth.

It's possible that you think me cruel. You can keep your opinions. This is a dream. You can't be blamed for those. Can you even imagine something so small wiggling down your throat? The sensation, what must that feel like? If anything I did her a favor. I'll never know the pleasure, not consciously.

Let me move on. I found that watching her struggle, gag and try coughing the funnel out of her throat started to annoy me So I put a clothespin over her nose. She started crying. She gives me a look as if she's truly sorry, but we know that isn't true.

This is when I reveal the second bag, the one that simply has pieces. Ears, toes, the tongue, fingers, you know. All covered with little friends. Now, this is when the funnel begins to shake, followed by a gurgling, choking sound. It's cute but annoying, that problem is solved by a downward shove that scrapes her teeth.

Now for the pieces. I take an ear, the tongue, a finger, a toe or two and drop them into the funnel. Then I add the leftovers, remaining toes, fingers and lip skin. I thought of adding the last piece, but decided against it. She's had enough of that already.

Of course not everything went down, but it does soon enough. I make sure of that. I force every single bit and piece of him down into the funnel and watch events unfold. She was choking like a streetwalker, eyes bulging, body convulsing, then comes vomit. It doesn't shoot out crazily like some 80's film. Instead it bubbles and rises to the top of the funnel. A mixture of red and yellow but not quite orange, little friends swimming around like children. Eventually she dies of her own vomit. Which is, in a way, fitting.

Now for the children, formerly ours, now mine. Of course I would not, could not harm them. What would that make me? You know, a monster. No, I would never do that. My children have not betrayed me. They could not, would not, betray me. The children, as I have mentioned, are innocent. So, then comes the difficulties. I had to explain the smell in the kitchen, describing to them what happened, why we had to move and finally, to find a new job. That last one wouldn't be difficult. And of course, I wouldn't actually explain the details of what happened to their mother. The world is hateful enough. Why scar them?

I don't really like lying to children, much less my own, but sometimes you have to, to protect their innocence. We parents do it all the time: Santa Claus, the Tooth Fairy, the Bogeyman, etc. Why the bogeyman? Because we always tell our children that he doesn't exist. That he's a figment of their imagination. But we parents know that isn't true. We all have had at least one in our lifetimes. Thankfully, I took care of mine, in a dream.

\*\*\*

Much like my friends, a family sticks together. Bumps in the road can be overcome. Unless of course they ruin your car, but that's why you take it nice and slow. Careful, always careful, that's the way.

Foolish as it is, it does tempt the mind to speed over those bumps and let your vigor do the work, speeding right over and landing in a heap, bouncing in the vehicle. The landing like falling from the apex of a mountain, the children would say "roller coaster!"

On your way to that bump, you press down on the gas and throw caution to the wind. In the air you feel freedom. Next to you your wife's eyes bulge and her teeth clench. Behind you the children raise their arms and scream. That big bump sends the car sky high and what goes up must eventually come crashing down.

Now, if only we all had the courage to follow through. Wouldn't that be something? I regret to admit that cowardice runs in the family. Unfortunate, I know.

Nevertheless, I'm happy with life. I'm happy with my children, my wife and even the reality of her lover. Everybody's happy here. We are happy little maggots. All happily crawling and eating together. How's life been for you? I really can't complain.

Reality's funny, you know? It almost feels like a dream sometimes. It can in fact be that if we want. Waking up doesn't mean much. You can always decide to dream again, to reawaken an urge. For now, we live. That's all we can do, until we don't. Honestly, anger's probably the dumbest impulse next to infidelity. I'm sure you'd agree.

# Warm Hugs (SJ Townend)

It had been a crisp night, a numb-toe night, the night the staff nurse found Michael swaddled in a blanket on the steps of the hospital. His cries had pierced the darkness whilst the whiteness of her exhalations had frayed into the cold. He went straight in the incubator box—not that a baby would remember any of this—and the nurse went straight home to her family.

Michael, reformed alcoholic, now lives in a hostel for men with seventeen idiots that he cannot stand. A man of few words and fewer actions, his hair now lies tangled and brindle underneath his red beanie hat where once it used to lie flat and black. He keeps himself to himself. Not that anyone else would want him.

Today, the council put a sign up on the bench where he spends his working week. It says: "DO NOT FEED THE PIGEONS," so he doesn't and rather than spending his last ninety-six pence on a loaf of cheap sliced white from the corner shop—breakfast, lunch and dinner, ends for the birds—he purchases a can of Special Brew instead. He cracks back the ring pull, inhales the welcoming fumes of a long forgotten friend, a familiar halitosis and glugs down the brown poison whilst trying to figure out why he's wasted six weeks on sobriety.

Sip. Sup. The juice is gone and he has no money left for more. He sits in the sunshine running his tongue through the gap in his mouth where he used to have a tooth, tasting the bittersweet residue of the old pal he has sunk until all the thrusting and probing yields is the flavour of sour saliva and mild gingivitis once more. He sits and stands and stands and sits. The pigeons won't come near him. He asks passersby for spare change or cigarettes but all he is offered is: "hugs, not drugs," from some white kid with dreadlocks who's pushing a neon e-scooter and wearing a Hypercolour t-shirt older than his own bones.

"Fuck off. No thanks," Michael replies, trying to hold it down-town. The posh kid shrugs his shoulders and scoots off for his vegan fry-up with Tarquin and Tallulah and their I-pads.

"Just want a four pack, that's all," says Michael to his one and only lead of the day, but his words are lost, with the birds, to the sky.

He crunches his long dead can with his laceless boot and kicks it under a bush. He bends and picks up a yellow lighter caked in dried mud and flicks and flicks and flicks the cog until his thumb blisters and until he gets the bastard to work. Bingo. Flames. He pockets his treasure and makes his way back to his room, wishing he had bought the bread instead. The back of his neck feels a little sunburnt and the pigeons didn't want to know at all.

*It's time*, he thinks, *for that warm hug,* so he pulls on a third sweater and slides his arms through lumberjack shirt sleeves. Bursting black and red tartan squares, like swollen prison bars, conceal his average, birdcage chest which is buried beneath. When each button fastens eventually and there's no more pop pop pop, he goes for a second button-

137

down number with a hood and wishes he had more clothing with zips.

He tries to put on more layers to keep out the wintery draft that only he feels on this balmy Tuesday. He gets to the bottom of the third drawer down and realises he's run out of clothing. Is he wrapped up well enough to keep the chill at bay? Most would say amply so, but Michael still feels the cold, there's something up with his insulation, a wind tunnel blowing through his core. He creeps out of his room on the second floor of the shared house-cum-hostel and listens with cupped hands against the plasterboard wall—is John in?

Big John, not One-Foot, that is.

Are any of his house mates in?

Mate is a broadly over-used term in Michael's world and he knows he doesn't have any real friends. But he doesn't care because people have eyes, don't they? And eyes can burn through layers; eyes can torch-beam through the black of midnight straight into his very centre. Eyes read minds. It's the probing eyes of others that keep trying to burrow into his soul and dig out the ancient wisdom that he's tucked up so deeply in there that even Michael can't quite fish it out.

No-one's home so he pushes open the door and enters Big John's room. It looks a lot like Michael's: semen-marbled sheets, army surplus, dander and dust—except it's filled with John's stuff instead of his and the sink is on the other side of the door. As Michael approaches John's wardrobe, he walks a bit like a robot. The layers he's already got on are keeping his arms away from his flank and are prising his legs and knees away from each other just a little further than is acceptably comfortable—a little further than nature intended. His joint mobility is somewhat compromised by clothing more than it is normally by his myopathic, Special Brew gait, but he can still bend his arm just enough to open John's wardrobe door.

He paws off another two shirts from John's hangers and puts them on and squeezes on a further three trouser pairs. Big John's loose fit jeans fit perfectly now on Little Mike. And, as luck so happens, it turns out John is a fan of hats too. Michael manages to get them all on his head at once. With his new lighter, he sets fire to a ball of newspaper that once contained batter bits and scraps from the chippy across the way and drops it onto the collection of other hoarded litter John appears to have collected at the foot of his bed.

He shuffles back to his own room, flops onto the cheap mattress, a ninety-degree slap, and lies amongst the rumpled sheets and waits for the heating to kick in. It must have been an hour at least since he broke the padlock on the Operations' Unit door and flipped the thermostat up to max. He's starting to sweat and feel thirsty now, so he turns his head away to avoid facing the lime-scaled tap which is shouting at him. It's shouting loudly words of water and ice and crisp weather so he screws his eyes closed too and puts his fingers in his ears to block out the noise of the sink—not that it works; it hasn't done since the start of his tenancy.

When the sink quietens down, Michael pulls a hand from his ear and picks blindly at the flaking paint on the wall as the temperature in his room soars with the pigeons. He pulls up his bed sheets and the extra duvet he scrounged from the soup kitchen and lies and lies and waits as his heart rate starts to creep up and his throat starts to feel like the desert. In his mind he sees the brown poison in a glass on a picnic table, calling out at him to drink, but he's going nowhere, he's drinking nothing, except lashings of stout-sour memories of probing eyes staring down on him and cold stethoscopes pressing forever on his young chest. The memories keep on flooding in, like the urine flooding his bed.

The flies above him can't get out as he's closed up all of the windows. He opens his eyes and stares deliriously upwards and tries to snap out of his Special Brew Dream by interpreting the stop-start patterns that the flies are making in the air as they communicate with him in jerky semaphore. He can hear the boiler in the hall way straining and clunking and so is his heart.

It's very warm now.

Fucking hot, in fact.

He goes right under the duvet and pulls it in tight at the sides to keep the liquor vampires and the pigeons and the nurses and the care staff out and he closes his eyes and thinks of the mother that never hugged him and waits for the fire to spread.

First published by BRISTOL NOIR MAGAZINE (2021)

# Four Sided Bottle (Rickey Rivers Jr.)

Jonathan awoke in his bed, confused. The bed sheets were wrapped around his lower half. A naked woman was next to him, her head beneath a pillow. Her skin seemed to shine from the sunlight peering into the bedroom.

Something happened last night but he couldn't remember what. His head hurt. He stood up and nearly fell over before stumbling into the bathroom. Once there he splashed water onto his face and looked into the mirror. He was there, but he didn't like what he saw.

Jonathan yanked open the medicine cabinet and searched, then grabbed a pill bottle. Vomit rose up, came out of his mouth and into the sink. He sat down on the toilet seat and waited for his head to steady. Then he put the pills in his mouth.

"These are aspirins," he told himself. Then he swallowed them.

From the bathroom he could see his bedroom. The woman was still there. As far as he could tell she hadn't moved at all. He stood up, slow with shaky legs, balancing himself on the vomit stained sink. Then, for the first time, he approached his own bed with caution.

"Hey," he said, nudging her.

She didn't move.

He turned the woman over and looked at her. Her face was gone. There was a blank sheet of skin where her face should have been. The woman then moved in a slow manner and said something somehow that sounded pleasant. He could hear her words and understand that they came from her, but nothing otherwise told him that she had said anything.

On impulse he said good morning.

The woman sat up, stretched and made an audible yawn.

"Do I know you?" said Jonathan.

The woman made a laughing sound. "You don't remember?"

He shook his head.

"How insulting." She stood up.

Jonathan moved aside to let her pass. The woman went to the bathroom and Jonathan followed.

"Can you remind me?" he said. "My head hurts. I'm not sure what happened last night."

The woman splashed water onto her no-face, drank some somehow then spat it out back into the sink. She turned her back to the mirror and leaned on the sink. "You really don't remember?"

"No," he said.

"Well, what if I don't remember either?"

Jonathan put a hand to his head. It hurt to think. "What do you mean - you don't remember?"

"Just like you," she said.

There was a pause. He looked at her, trying to read her lack of face then he straight out asked her. "Why can't I see what you look like?"

"That's rude," she said, walking back into the bedroom.

"I'm just trying to understand," said Jonathan.

142

The woman sat on the bed. "My looks didn't seem to bother you yesterday."

"We slept together?"

"No duh."

"And you remember that?"

"I woke up here naked... so yeah."

It did make sense, he thought.

"Besides, what's the big deal?" she said.

"What do you mean? I can't remember anything."

"Same here."

"And why aren't you upset about that?"

The woman tilted her head. "I don't know," she said. "I feel like I shouldn't be. It was consensual."

Jonathan sat next to her. Both of them were silent. Clothes were thrown all around the room. The bathroom door was wide open. The smell of vomit was fresh in the air. A sad feeling came over him. He felt aimless. He felt he'd lost control, not only of the current situation, but also of his life.

He stood up and reached for his pants on the floor. He nearly fell over but instead made a wobbly recovery. The woman shook her head.

Jonathan reached into his pants pocket with unsure hands. "Where's my wallet?"

"Are you asking me?" said the woman.

"I'm just-" he stopped himself. "I don't know my name anymore and you're here, so..."

The woman laughed. "You're Jonathan."

"Oh? Okay," he knew that, part of that. "But I still need my ID."

"Sure," she said. "Check the dresser drawers, check under the bed, check everywhere else, my love."

He did so. He started with the drawers then he searched under the bed. His wallet was there. It was like she knew.

"Here!" he said, holding the wallet high.

"Good," she said. "Is there money in there for me?"

"You're a prostitute?"

"...that was a joke, Jonathan."

"I'm sorry, my head..." his voice trailed, he didn't recognized jokes anymore. Besides, nothing was funny. He couldn't remember the last time he laughed. Jonathan looked into his wallet and saw that money was there, his ID was there, bank cards too, and everything else that should be there.

"All good?" she asked.

"Yeah," he said.

"Great, now what?"

"Well," he put his wallet on the nearby dresser, "since you remember my name, how about giving me yours?"

"Since you don't remember, it really doesn't matter."

"Yes it does."

"What I mean is, I can basically tell you any name and you'd believe it."

"...I guess that's true."

"Sure it is!"

"But that's not fair, I told you my name."

"No, I remembered your name."

"Yeah but-" he paused, "If we just slept together..."

She waited. Jonathan was thinking. His head was throbbing.

"Go on," she said.

"Then why shouldn't you tell me your name?"

"Maybe I don't want you to know?"

"Then why sleep with me?"

"Why do anything? Look, is this really a big deal?"

"It feels like it should be."

"Why don't we just go our separate ways and never speak to each other again?"

That sounds good, he thought. Now he wanted nothing to do with her. "Fine, okay. Just leave me here with amnesia."

"Amnesia's not a synonym for a hangover."

"I'm hungover? I don't drink."

"Come on, now." The woman stood, pretended to wobble like him and scrambled together her clothes. She got dressed in front of him. She took her time too, almost mocking him.

"Well, it's been fun."

"You're leaving?"

"Sure."

"Can you just… tell me more about me?"

"What do I look like?"

A woman without a face, he thought. "You know what? Never mind, just leave!"

"Well, thank you for giving me permission." she scoffed and went to the front door.

"Hey, I'm sorry," he said. Truly he was. He didn't know this woman to be so rude.

"Don't worry about it." The woman grabbed the doorknob and stopped like she was waiting for him to remember something.

"Why did I drink?" he said. Not to her, to himself.

"Because that's what you like to do when things happen in your life that you can't control. That's what you told me."

"I don't remember saying that."

"And you told me about your wife, your job and other things that don't matter."

"My wife…?" Jonathan surveyed his own hands. There wasn't a ring or any indentation of a ring.

"Jon boy, remember when I said I could tell you any name and you'd believe it?"

"…I don't remember that."

"Of course you don't. Go back to sleep. Maybe you'll remember yourself in the morning."

The woman opened the door and walked out. Beyond the door Jonathan saw images. Geometry seemed to reconstruct, forming a destination for the woman. He stood there teetering. Then he spun on his way back to bed. He couldn't make it. He fell forward and landed in front of it instead. With lazy arms he pulled himself up and into it.

Tomorrow, he told himself, tomorrow I'll remember.

He blinked heavy eyelids and saw his bedside clock. The hands were spinning. They spun so fast he could barely see them. His head was hurting. The pills weren't aspirin. The clock hands spun invisible. Then he closed his eyes and everything went black.

Maybe upon waking he'd remember his job, the previous night, and the night before that? Who knew anything but the no-face woman? She had lied about not remembering anything, but why would she lie? Who was she to him?

Jonathan fell asleep. During his sleep he dreamed. He saw himself in a room. Around him were other people. They sat in chairs in a circle with him. They all had a no-face. One of the no-face people cried. Another shook their head. One had their head to the floor. Soon a no-face close to him spoke "The first step?"

What was it?

"Do you remember the first step?"

No.

"Admittance."

When he woke the sun was still up. Had it been the same day? He couldn't remember the no-face woman but he did remember the dream. The no-faces there had been disappointed. He stumbled out of bed and headed to the bathroom. He was thirsty so he drank water from the sink faucet. Then he reached into the medicine cabinet and grabbed the bottle of not-aspirin. He contemplated for a moment, but his reflection made the choice.

Jonathan poured the pills down the drain and threw the pill bottle into the trash. He went to the dresser and picked up his wallet, inside was the card with the number. He grabbed the card and went to his phone. The volume on the phone had been turned down. He saw the amount of missed calls and cursed.

Card in one hand and phone in the other he dialed the number. When the person on the other end answered he held his breath.

"Hello?" said the person.

"Yes, my name is Jonathan... Jonathan Larson, I need help."

"Again, Mr. Larson?"

"Yes, I'm not well."

"Again, Mr. Larson?"

"Please"

"Have you taken your medicine?"

"That wasn't medicine."

"Are you sure, Mr. Larson?"

"Please, send help. I took aspirin, but I don't think it was aspirin."

"Any strange women in your bed, Mr. Larson?"

"No." He looked to be sure. "T-there was a woman here. She's gone now. She was with me the other night."

"Then what happened?"

"I don't know. I guess I was drunk."

"But you don't drink Mr. Larson."

"I know I don't, that's why I need help. Call a doctor."

"Are you sure, Mr. Larson?"

"Yes!"

The other end of the phone went quiet. Jonathan kept it to his ear. "Hello?" he said.

The woman on the other end was speaking with someone. They were whispering. Soon there was laughter and many voices on the other end.

"Stop it," said Jonathan. "Stop laughing."

But they didn't stop. They kept laughing, men and woman, their voices congealing.

"I just want some help," said Jonathan.

"I just want some help," said a mocking woman.

"Why won't you help me? What did I do wrong?"

"You can start with the pills," said someone. The phone went dead.

"Hello?" said Jonathan. No answer. "Hello?"

Jonathan threw the phone to the floor. "Fine, I'll leave. I'm sick of this."

He collected himself and set out toward the front door. He opened it and felt a rush of traffic, lights, buildings and many shadows of people going their own way, some walking lengthwise toward twilight roofs.

"Put on some clothes on!" said someone.

Jonathan looked down. He was naked. He was cold.

"Look at the small man," said someone else.

The people laughed.

"No," said Jonathan, "I need some help."

The laughter kept going. Traffic flew past him. The buildings elongated, some began to lean as if listening.

"I took some pills I shouldn't have. I'm sorry, but I did. Can someone help me?"

Strange reflective birds began to swirl before settling. The loudness of the city now mixed with the cawing of unseen crows, the croaking of unseen frogs, the bleating of faraway sheep, them all a noisy crowd.

Jonathan fell to his knees and curled into a ball, still hearing the sounds bombard. Them all reminded him of simpler times, the mobile spinning above the crib, more controlled in nature, his parents seeing him this way, unaware of the outside world, him now small, shaken.

"Jonathan," said his mother. "Those pills aren't for you."

He remembered this, his mother's voice, the only voice that mattered. In his head he went to her, hoping to see her again, her actual face; the one beyond the pills. He wanted so badly to see her. Then he wanted his wife. Then he wanted children. Someone, anyone to talk to in the now, as he became the child person in the place he always was. Nurses went scrambling, no one had answers, much less care for prescriptions.

# Deep Town (Dona Fox)

She's out here somewhere; I feel her presence like a beacon. I've always felt her; the moment she was conceived I felt her stirring inside me. I didn't need lines on a stick as proof. After she was born, I knew when she woke in her crib, I was instantly on alert. When she went away to school I'd show up when she needed to come home after a heartbreak or a failure (which were few). Once she'd married, I felt every blow from his fists.

Tonight, the only reason I'd brought such a large handbag was for the knife and now I wish I hadn't brought any sort of purse at all. I could have stuffed the knife down the side of my skirt, or taken a smaller one and put it in my shoe. But I had to have the butcher knife, didn't I? The biggest one off the rack. I must have been thinking of what I would do to Anders if he accosted me.

I'd planned so well, why hadn't I changed my shoes? My heels click-clacked sexily on the pavement, echoing against the empty office buildings as if I were sending out a signal to ensure everyone noticed me, the helpless woman, running through the deserted streets of downtown Sacramento at 3 a.m., dodging the crows' droppings that pock-marked the icy sidewalks.

I could hear the unhomed people stirring in the alleys, then the quiet shuffling as they followed me as if attracted by my purse—a beacon which called every waking shadow to me, perhaps they thought I had money, which I didn't. Well, not much.

Nevertheless, my heart pounded in the empty cavity of my chest. I walked faster.

There was one car—too expensive for me to recognize or name—that seemed to be circling the blocks I ran through, the dark sedan stayed with me, windows down, filling the night with a scent, both familiar and exotic along with the sound of smooth jazz that created a presence that was almost reassuring. But I wouldn't turn, I didn't dare to steal a look. I was here to bring my daughter home.

Then they were on me.

The miasma of the unbathed froze me in place as they surrounded me. I had no way out as they closed in; I held my purse under my arm, tight against my body. Their eyes were not drugged nor crazed, simply tired as they held out their hands in a silent request for food, for money. I'd seen the expression before, along with the empty palms, in a dozen different countries—on the television before I turned the channel, in my magazines as I flipped the page away and they reached out to me through the mail which I quickly recycled.

I closed my eyes.

"Rafe. Back them off then come here." A man's voice—dark and alluring as the memory of melted brown sugar, butter, and honey in a cinnamon roll—poured from the gently idling car.

I opened my eyes as an impossibly tall young man in a black hoodie and white sneakers stepped out of the crowd then turned his thin back to me. "Listen up. She got nothin'. Best bet's down to St. Joseph's. Leave now. Hurry. Line's forming." He

152

made swooshing gestures with his bony hands. Grumbling, the crowd disbursed.

The young man who answered to the name of Rafe ran to the dark car and bent down to the window. He nodded several times then he approached me cautiously holding out his large hands palms up and out toward me, a calming gesture. As if I were a wild animal that needed to be gentled.

"Darcy wants to know if he can give you a ride back to where you belong." I watched his Adam's apple bob as he spoke.

"No, I'm where I belong tonight, or close to it, I believe," I said.

"If we may be so bold as to ask," he spoke slowly, carefully, hands clasped tightly together as if the short speech was a difficult, memorized effort; he looked back at the dark sedan as if for reassurance that he was saying the words correctly, "what are you doing here and how may we assist you?"

"I've lost my daughter."

"Oh. A little girl?" Another quick glance at the dark sedan. "She's out here alone on the streets? There's no time to waste!" Rafe was bouncing on his toes.

"She's my little girl," I couldn't keep the warble out of my voice now, "but she's not a child—she's thirty-three."

"Oh." Rafe came down off his toes.

"Her husband, he was cruel."

"He beat her? Bruises then? A sad thing."

"Yes."

"Aren't they all!" Rafe ran back to the car and leaned into the window again for a quick conversation, half hand gestures, ending with nods as he backed away. Rafe returned to stand beside me, but facing the sedan.

A muscular arm stretched from the car's window and a gloved hand reached into the air. A large bird fell from the sky and landed on the glove. The man brought his hand-with the bird clinging to its-back, into the car, closed the window and drove away.

"That's Marty, the bird, I mean. Falcon, eagle, I can't remember which. He's chasing off the crows. City pays us. Come on then, I'll show you where the sad women go but I won't be going. Too dangerous. Pay me." He held out one palm.

"You want money?"

"Yes. What you can spare. Half now and half when I show you the door."

I gave him a few bills then I let him take my hand and trotting, he pulled me zig-zagging through the city streets until we came to a deep pit right in the middle of blocks and blocks filled with gleaming high-rise office buildings that seemed to be constructed of nothing but glass and mirrors from which light reflected from one to the other, cracked and shone into the sky. We walked down a thick plank into the pit until darkness enveloped us.

"You have a cell?" he said. I nodded. "Light up that wall." The wall he indicated ran the entire side of the pit; it was built of crumbling concrete blocks and old red bricks. "Yep," he said, "years ago, way back-after the dinosaurs, I think. The city flooded-

154

all the time-so they raised the whole dang place up- the whole town-and started over, but higher. Ain't that sumthin'? There's your door. I'll take my other half now."

Stunned, I put my hands on the wall. I moved my light so it shone on the dark doorway he indicated then I pressed a few more bills into his hand. I didn't let go. "Come with me."

He pulled away, leaving the bills behind. Most of them fluttered to the ground, but others caught in an odd gust of wind and circled like the crows.

"No way, ma'am."

"Then I'm not going in there. This is a trick," I suggested warily, knowing full well I'd walk through an alligator infested swamp by myself to save my daughter.

"Say what you want," he sighed, "but I know you're goin' in. Don't get involved with anything you see in there. You can't be everybody's savior. And watch out for the young 'uns out here if you decide not to go in." He spun and trotted away, calling over his shoulder, "no hard feelings you didn't pay me."

Rafe left me in the silent city in the cold pit looking into the eye of the yearning hollow that opened under the sidewalk. Circling crows broke the spell with a sudden noisy gathering in the sky above me and the resultant droppings.

I ducked under the lip of the doorway. I tried to make out a logic to the crows' flight, to their screams. I didn't see the figures come up on me until the knife was already at my neck.

"Drop your bag, slip off your shoes and your coat," the one behind me growled, pressing the knife against my throat.

"Where's your phone?" The edge of the blade burned as it sliced. The scent of rotten oranges with a tinge of sour sweat burned my eyes; I wouldn't soon forget the blade wielder's odor.

"In my purse," I squeaked.

They held my elbows and, like a zombie, I stepped out of my shoes. My body was frozen but my mind was racing, should I twirl and smash my purse into the thief? Should I slip out of my coat and throw it over his head? No, he wasn't alone. I watched too much television. I did exactly as requested and prayed I would be allowed to live.

My body began to tremble and I couldn't catch my breath.

I came to face down, mouth full of the gritty dirt of the pit, my hands grasping forward toward the doorway, as if I wanted to crawl into the dirt and hide. I did. I was freezing. I had no shoes, no coat and no purse. That meant I had no knife and no money to bribe or buy my way through the tunnel. If I had to rely on my wits to find my daughter I might be in trouble. No, I wouldn't think of it that way; my load had been lifted, I could travel better now, I was lighter, faster on my feet. I threw back my shoulders and walked into the shadows.

The tunnel was cold, icy water flowed over my feet. My eyes weren't adjusting to the lack of light; maybe there was no way for the human eye to adapt to this much darkness.

Bodies hurtling through the tunnel brushed against me, sometimes brutally. I reached for the wall to my right. Immediately my hand was coated with cobwebs; tiny spiders crawled up inside my sleeve and from there they sped to the roots of my hair and every warm, damp part of my body. I tried to brush them off, but soon I'd feel the tiny feet all over me again. I needed to hold onto the wall or the stampeding bodies would knock me down. I gritted my teeth and tried to brush the spiders off my right arm with my left hand as quick as they arrived. Pretty soon I had a rhythm and it wasn't so bad—much as, I suppose people in the dark ages got used to their fleas.

But I wasn't making any progress—was this going to go on forever—I couldn't take it—icy water running over my feet, brutal bodies jostling me on the left, fighting the tiny spiders on my right, the total darkness. I was about to shriek and run out of the tunnel with the hurtling bodies when I saw a dim glow up ahead. I let go of the wall and ran to the light.

It was a tiny candle, like a birthday candle, about to go out. Next to it lay a boy beneath a large concrete block. He gave me a pathetic crooked smile and licked his bloody lips.

"Help me, please," he croaked, "board, rock, fulcrum?" he nodded toward the wall.

One glance in the direction he indicated and I understood what he wanted—a thick plank was leaning against the wall and there were a number of different size rocks around the space, he wanted me to use the plank and one of the rocks to create a

157

fulcrum and lift the concrete off him. I had to assume he still had the wherewithal to squirm out once the block was raised.

I did as he requested but I had to put my foot on the fulcrum and bend down next to him to pull him out. My eyes began to water—he smelled of rotten oranges and sour sweat. This was the boy who'd held the knife to my throat! When I released him would he harm me; would he revert to character and turn on me like the snake brought in from the cold by the farmer in the Aesop's fable?

I had the power to help him and it was the right thing to do; I pulled him out and let the block fall.

"I remember you," I said.

He bent over, catching his breath, then he raised his head and looked me in the eye. "Rafe double-crossed you, never should have sent you in here." He nodded several times then gulped the stale tunnel air. Finally, holding his chest, doubled-over, he staggered away as the light winked out.

A smooth voice circled around me, "that was fortunate. You were very brave; he could have turned on you but you chose to do the right thing. I'll help you. Take my hand." The voice was mellow, the hand encased in a thick leather glove.

"Are you the man who chases the crows away? Who are you?" I asked.

Laughter filled the tunnel. "Yes, though I have a hawk with me tonight, I am called the Falconer."

The tunnel seemed to be closing in on us. There was no one but us in the space now; no rushing bodies passing on the left, no tiny spiders on the right. And now, if I wanted, I could touch both sides, both walls of the passage.

Finally we had to go single file, the Falconer behind me, hands on my shoulders, guiding me. Then, hands on my back, gently pushing me.

"I'm starting to feel a little claustrophobic," I said, trying to turn but finding the tunnel too tight, the movement impossible.

"You want to find your daughter, don't you?"

"Yes, more than anything, and I know she's near."

"Then you must keep moving." The Falconer gave me a shove and I fell into a very small tunnel.

A gate slammed shut behind me. I felt betrayed.

I was lying on my stomach. Small, slick bodies covered with hair moved against mine. I felt the prickle of spidery whiskers, the lash of hard bare tails and the poke of cold, wet noses. I could hear running footsteps on the sidewalk above me. I tried to turn. The space was too small and my furry roommates protested by piercing me with their spiky teeth.

Finally, I turned so that I was on my back. I pounded on what must have been the bottom of the sidewalk above me until a crack formed. Bits of cement began to fall into my eyes and mouth. What if the whole sidewalk collapsed onto me?

My body went numb; the muscles in my arms and legs seemed to freeze. I couldn't move. I wanted to scream but I had no breath.

I stopped and stretched my bare feet to the gate the Falconer slammed shut behind me. I felt every inch of the wire mesh, but it was too strong for me to break. I felt around the edges until I found the latch. The cement the latch was set in had begun to crumble. If I picked at it with my toenails, could I loosen it and remove the gate? Would I bring down the sidewalk? That would be dangerous if the gate is all that's keeping the pavement from falling down on me.

I hadn't tried scooting forward, following the tunnel. I tried that now and I was looking through to a vent into the sidewalk about two yards above me. But it was right there. I could see the soles of the shoes of the people as they stepped on the metal grids. The noise of the light rail as it ran to one side of me was thunderous and sounds from the cars that drove oh so close to me and in the nearby lanes echoed against the buildings—all night noises unbearably amplified in the empty canyons of the office buildings.

But the sidewalk, the people—they were right there—right above me. When I saw someone, I screamed until my chest was sore. My screams were lost in the cacophony.

The crystal tears that cracked in my eyes sharpened my vision; I could see the top of the nearest building as clear as if I had my glasses. Movement of the hawk chasing the crows drew my eye, when the birds moved on, two figures remained on the roof.

One was my daughter. I knew her shape, the way she held her head and moved her body. I knew her-but not well enough I realized. Was she hiding from him? Or, heaven forbid—was she there to jump?

The other—at the farthest corner of the roof—larger, massive with a tiny head—arms so muscled he couldn't lay them next to his body—or was that an affectation? Yes, that was him. The brute. Her husband. Perhaps he hadn't noticed her yet. But there was no time to lose. Was he there to harm her?

I pushed forward until—whoosh. I slid down another tunnel and landed in a bright and airy room filled with women, children, and men—all with bruises in varying states of recovery.

They gasped as I landed, looked me over and pulled away as if I didn't belong.

"I've lost my daughter." My voice was loud and clear.

One person broke from the crowd and stepped forward. "Did you beat her?" she said.

"Well—no, it was her husband."

"Why did you pause? Did you beat her?"

"I don't understand what you're asking," I said.

"It was a simple question, yes or no. Did you beat her?"

Scenes only I could see covered the walls. Black and white images flickered on the television behind my little girl and me. I pulled her by one arm as I slapped her face then I struck her with a metal spoon wherever I could find an uncovered area of skin, a tender spot. Bombs exploded on the television screen, tanks blew up in a jungle as she screamed, the newscaster talked with tears in his eyes and I pinched her mouth to shut her up.

It was only recently I found her lying on the carpet of her home, bruised, several teeth clutched in her hand. On the giant television the war in

161

Afghanistan raged. The screen was paused to a scene of bodies piled in the streets. My little girl, not so little now, reached out and laid her bloody palm across a woman's hand. Things have fallen apart; you're not alone, I'll die with you.

Now the people in the room under the city all closed in, waiting for my answer.

"I'm looking for my daughter; I've lost my daughter. I've gone through a lot to find her. I think I saw her outside on the roof. How can I get out of here? It's urgent."

"I imagine she isn't outside; she's more likely living deep. Come back to Deep Town when you're ready to talk honestly."

The crowd surrounded me, cawing like the flock of crows that comes out to play from dusk to dawn in the winter in downtown Sacramento and the next I knew I was standing in the icy pit; the low winter sun hitting the mirrored glass of the high-rises.

I didn't see anyone on the roof. Had it been my imagination? A view of the future?

I could go back into the fun-house, start from the beginning looking for my daughter and Deep Town again, or I could try to walk home barefoot on the icy sidewalks and think about the woman's question and its deeper meaning.

When did I lose my daughter?

Was I a harsh mommy? Did I teach her to love a bully?

I'd make it up to her and I wouldn't lose her again.

I shook my head and ran out of the pit. The office building was open, workers streamed in to their jobs, fortunately no id's were required and, this being California, no one noticed my lack of shoes, they didn't even look at me as I pressed the elevator button for the roof.

As I exited on the roof, I considered my options; I found only one elegant solution to my daughter's problem.

There she was, the rising sun shining on her head so bright I could smell the baby shampoo in her hair. I could imagine the scent of her scalp after a day of hard play in the summer sunshine. I ran to her, to nuzzle her hair and I put my arms around her-tight.

Her rough husband, the beast, came slowly around the corner, his eyes, usually blank and pitiless as a reptile now blazed with fury. How could the same God who made my daughter have made this man?

As the sun rose and day dawned the hawk was circling, its intentions unclear.

"I love you, my darling daughter. I will stay with you, hold you, and love you for the rest of our lives." I kept her in my embrace as I stepped off the roof. I thought it was a glorious solution.

She died.

Obviously, I survived. That hadn't been my plan.

I woke up in the Falconer's home in the woods. He brought me the newspapers. My daughter died on impact. She felt no pain. Her husband was arrested for her murder; an open and shut case.

I understand now the Falconer didn't betray me in the tunnel; sometimes we need a push to get on with the hard parts of our lives. He said it wasn't easy, he wanted to bring me home with him the moment we met.

The Falconer wants me to stay with him and I believe I will. I'm addicted to his scent, both familiar and exotic along with the sound of smooth jazz—it sets a reassuring atmosphere—but it's always played softly in this home, to ensure that I can always hear the falconer, 'lest I fall apart again.

# What Doesn't Kill You (Michelle Ann King)

Roasting beef, fresh vegetables. Real coffee. Wonderful aromas that she'd almost forgotten.

The meal had torn a massive hole in their rations, but Olivia didn't care about that. Robert was home. That was the only thing that mattered.

'Come and sit down,' Carol said. 'The food's ready.'

Olivia turned, surprised to see her set only two plates on the dining table. 'What about Robert?'

'He's in the bath.'

'Still? Well, he must be clean by now. I'll go and get him.'

'No.' Carol's hand shot out and gripped her wrist. 'Leave him be. Sit down. Eat your dinner.'

Olivia stared at her. 'What's the matter?'

Carol let go of her arm and looked away. 'They said it was a chemical spill, the first time. An accident. Do you remember that?'

Olivia frowned. 'Yes, but what's—'

'We watched it on the news,' Carol went on. 'There were people being rescued and evacuated, like it was a flood or an earthquake. Everyone packed into community centres and church halls, being given cups of tea and wrapped in blankets donated by Oxfam. They cleared the area for five miles. Five miles. Can you imagine trying that now?'

She sat down at the table and looked at her plate, but didn't pick up her knife and fork.

Olivia put a hand on her shoulder. 'Don't,' she said gently. 'I know it looks bad, but they're going to figure it out. It's going to be okay.'

Carol shook her off. Her eyes glistened. 'It was a mistake,' she said. 'A baby. It's too much. Too much pressure.'

Olivia put a hand instinctively, protectively, on her stomach. 'What do you mean? Why would you say that?'

Finally, Carol raised her head and looked Olivia in the eye. 'You still don't get it, do you?'

The kitchen clock ticked, overly loud in the small room. Gooseflesh pricked Olivia's arms and she tried to rub some warmth back into them. 'Get what?'

'Why he came home tonight. Why they let him.'

'No, I don't. What are you talking about?'

'It's getting worse, you must know that. We all know it, even if we don't want to face it. Those gas explosions in Birmingham? The warehouse fire in Glasgow, the riots in Coventry? They're stories. Cover-ups. They want people to believe those things, because you can put out a fire and you can break up a riot. But there's nothing anyone can do about a Blight.'

Carol pushed her plate away. A drop of congealed gravy slid off the side.

The smell of meat, warm and rich, soured in Olivia's nostrils. 'What's wrong with you? This is supposed to be a special night.'

Carol's eyes were flat and empty. 'It's a goodbye. Don't you see, Olivia? Don't you understand? Robert, all the others—they've practically been prisoners in that lab. Why would they suddenly give them time off? Now, when things are worse than ever? I'll tell you: because they know there's no point in trying any more, that's why. They've given up. They know it's over.'

Olivia shook her head. 'I don't know what you're talking about,' she said. 'I'm going to get Robert.'

'Don't,' Carol said, but her voice had lost all its force.

Olivia got up and went to the bathroom. The door was closed, a piece of notepaper taped at eye level.

I'm sorry, the note said. I wanted us to go together, but I just couldn't do it. I hope you can find your own way and that you'll forgive me. I love you.

There was a smudge of ink, then it continued on the line underneath:

Olivia, call the police.

Don't come in.

\*\*\*

Olivia sat on the bed and stared at the pattern on the wallpaper—slender green sprigs against a silver background—as if it might reveal some secret, or explain how any of this had happened. Maybe tell her what she was supposed to do next.

'I wanted us to go together,' she said. Her tongue felt too large for her mouth, the words awkward and slow. 'That's what he said. Is that what he really came home to do? Kill me? Kill our baby?' She let out a long, juddering breath. 'Is it that bad? Is it really that bad?'

Carol stood in the doorway, leaning against the frame. 'He must have thought so.'

'Could you do it?' Olivia asked. 'What he couldn't? Could you kill me?'

Carol looked down at her. 'Do you want me to?'

Her voice held no expression, as if she were offering nothing more than to go and fetch the rations. *I heard we might be able to swap eggs for bread today. Do you want me to?*

The baby was a girl. Miranda, they'd decided. Miranda Jane.

'Could you have killed him?' she asked. 'Robert? Could you have taken that razor yourself, and cut his wrists?'

Carol said nothing for a long time. Then she closed her eyes. 'No.'

'No,' Olivia said. 'And I'm not going to kill my baby, either.' She struggled to her feet. 'I'm going outside.'

'It's not safe,' Carol said.

'Is it any safer in here? Death still got in, didn't it? This whole place stinks of it. Now, if you don't mind, please get the fuck out of my way.'

For a moment Carol stayed where she was, blocking the doorway. Then she did as she was told.

***

Olivia jabbed the call button on the landing and the lift responded straight away. One of the remaining advantages afforded to the families of government personnel: the building was looked after, the electricity supply maintained, security provided.

Or it used to be, anyway. Today, Olivia walked straight through the lobby. The guard's station was empty, the screens blank.

There had once been guards around the Blight outside, too. Road blocks, metal fences, warning signs, blank-faced men with guns. For your safety, do not proceed further.

But resources had been tested, then stretched, then snapped. So many people displaced, so much land lost. The priorities became simple: shelter, food, public order. Hurtling back down the slope of Maslow's hierarchy.

She stopped. Ahead, the edge of the Blight was clearly visible—the rubble and ruin, the grey weeds, the bones.

There was nothing left to stop anyone walking straight in, if they wanted. Go there, stay there. Die there. One less body to find space for, one less mouth to feed.

How many had made that choice?

Fewer buildings were lit up at night. The ration lines were getting shorter, not longer. She'd been pleased, to the extent that she'd noticed at all. More for her, for Carol. For Miranda.

She'd been so blind, for so long.

What was it like, to die in the Blight? To rot from the inside out?

Was it worse than sitting in a tub of hot water and watching it turn red?

Olivia picked her way through the broken glass and debris strewn across the road. This had been Coltswood Avenue, when she and Robert had first come to live here. A nice street, yellow brick terraces on one side and white-painted bungalows on the other. Cherry trees alternating with lampposts and shiny cars lined up in neat driveways.

Now the buildings were all in various stages of decay. Some had most of their walls standing and even part of a roof, but many had crumbled to nothing more than a pile of brick and dust. The cars were rusted sculptures of metal, looking like some kind of ancient industrial fossils. Unidentifiable bones crunched underfoot, sharp fragments poking through the thin soles of her shoes. It looked like the lost civilisation of a thousand years ago.

'Hello,' said a voice.

Olivia jumped, her heart jerking in her chest. The voice belonged to a child, maybe seven or eight years old. Tall, long-haired, dressed in dirty jeans and a sweatshirt that might once have been green. Girl or boy? She couldn't immediately tell.

'My name is Charlotte,' the child said, 'but you can call me Charlie if you like. My mum used to. What's your name? You have a very big belly.'

I'm Olivia.' She smiled and rested a hand on her stomach. 'And yes, I do. It's because I'm going

170

to have a baby, a little girl. She's going to be called Miranda.'

'That's a nice name,' Charlie said. 'Will she come and play with me?'

'I'm sure she'd like that, when she's old enough.' Olivia stepped forward. 'What are you doing here, Charlie? Where are your parents?'

Charlie turned and pointed to the remains of a house further down the street. 'I live down there. But I don't have parents any more. I used to have a mum and a granny, but they got sick. Now it's just me and Leo. He's my brother. He's fourteen. I'm seven and a half. That means I'm a little lady. How old are you? You look quite old. Leo is a teenager, which means he's a moody bastard. That's what my granny used to say, anyway.'

Olivia let out a choked laugh. Charlie grinned and bounced on the soles of her feet.

'And you live here?' Olivia said. 'You and Leo, you live here?'

'Yes. Would you like to come and see our house?'

Olivia hesitated and looked behind her. Already, it seemed like the start of the Blight was further away. She could go back, but to what?

She turned to Charlie and nodded. 'Okay.'

The girl smiled and took her hand.

Some of the lampposts had fallen, collapsed in the road or on top of the cars. Some still stood but were bent or swayed precariously. Some of the trees looked blasted, as if struck by lightning. Some appeared to have melted into a grey-brown sludge that dripped, in slow motion, off the kerb. A strange smell, half sweet and half rotten, drifted on the sluggish breeze.

'This used to be Mr and Mrs Bailey's house,' Charlie said. 'Ours fell down, so we couldn't stay there.'

She led Olivia to one of the soundest-looking houses, into what must once have been a living room. Shelves still lined one wall, some with tattered remnants of books stuck to them. A mossy, lumpy shape might have been a sofa, a fused mess of metal and wires might have been a television. Two sleeping bags, one plain blue and one with a pattern of cartoon pigs, were rolled out on the floor, between grey, twisted branches that had broken up through the patchy carpet. A glass jug rested nearby, three quarters full of greyish water.

'Mrs Bailey was called Mabel and she used to give me sweets,' Charlie said. 'But then they got sick too.' She picked something off the ground and held out her hand, palm upwards. 'Would you like some sweets?'

The objects she was holding could have been small fruits, once—plums, maybe. But now they were swollen, shiny and dark. Olivia recoiled.

'I know they look funny,' the girl said. 'But they're okay, really.' She popped one into her mouth, chewed and swallowed. 'I didn't like the food here much at first, but you get used to it.' She smiled, showing teeth stained black. 'Sometimes things don't taste very nice, but that means they're good for you. Like spinach. That's what my granny used to say.'

She broke off as something that looked like a large grey butterfly fluttered past. 'Ooh,' she said and grabbed it in one fist. Brown liquid trickled between her fingers onto the floor. She opened her hand and licked the palm.

Olivia stepped backwards, tripped over one of the questing roots and almost fell.

'Are you all right?' Charlie said. 'You don't look very well.'

'I'm fine,' she said. 'I just need to go and sit down for a while.' She found a smile. 'Charlie? Do you ever get sick, living here?'

The girl flashed Olivia a grin. Apart from those discoloured teeth, she looked healthy. Strong.

'No,' she said. 'Never. Will you come back later, after you've had your nap?'

Olivia swallowed hard, then nodded. 'Yes,' she said, 'I will.'

*** 

Carol held Olivia's hair back with one hand and rubbed her neck with the other. 'I thought you didn't want to die,' she said.

Olivia heaved again, but there was nothing left in her stomach. Her abdominal muscles felt shaky and sprung. 'I don't.'

'Then why the hell do you keep going out there? Think about what you're doing to yourself. To the baby.'

'Of course I'm thinking about that. It's all I ever think about.' She wiped her mouth with the back of her hand and struggled to her feet. 'You

173

haven't seen them, Carol. Charlie and Leo. The way they live is disgusting, yes, I'm not denying that. It's foul, the whole place. But it doesn't have to kill you. If they can do it, so can I. So can we.'

'You're out of your mind, girl.'

'What other choice do I have? You were right, it's getting bigger. Every day, more ground is gone. There's nowhere left to run and no-one's coming to fix it. You were right about that, too. So we have to find a way to live with it. That's the only choice we've got left.'

Carol put her hands on Olivia's shoulders and turned her to face the mirror. 'Look at yourself. Look at what it's doing to you.'

Olivia stared at the rough, grey patches on her face. At the sores. 'I'm still alive,' she said. The baby kicked, hard. 'And so's Miranda. That's what matters.' She smiled. 'What doesn't kill you, right?'

Carol flinched away from the reflection of her stained teeth and Olivia pulled out of her grip. It wasn't hard; there was no strength in Carol's hands. She'd been a big woman once, but now she was just bones jutting at sharp angles under sagging skin.

'Don't,' Carol said. 'Don't go back out there.'

Olivia paused in the doorway and looked back at her. 'I don't have to,' she said. 'Didn't you notice?' She ran a hand over the wall and the tile dissolved into a stream of thick dust. 'It's come to us.'

She turned and held out her hand. 'Come on. We should get out of here.'

Carol laughed, a weak but wild sound. 'And go where? There's nowhere left to run, remember?'

'We'll go to Charlie and Leo's. Take clothes, supplies, whatever we've got left. Some of it may survive. Come on, Carol. Now. We're on the fourth floor, here. If the building comes down fast, it'll be bad. We need to get outside.'

'Into the Blight.'

'Yes.'

Carol shook her head. 'No. I don't want to die like that.'

Olivia followed her gaze. 'That's an option,' she said, looking at the enamel bath. 'We still have razor blades. But I don't think it's as pleasant without the hot water.'

Carol didn't answer.

Olivia packed as much as she thought might be useful into a bag and waited outside the building. She waited for a long time, until the walls began to soften and slide. Then she shouldered her bag and walked away.

\*\*\*

Charlie met her at what used to be the garden wall. She scuffed at the dusty ground, kicked away a chunk of broken glass. Clean streaks showed through the dirt on her cheeks.

'What's wrong?' Olivia said. 'Charlie? What's the matter?'

'Leo,' Charlie said. It came out barely above a whisper.

'Leo? What's wrong with Leo?'

'He got sick.'

'Sick?' Olivia's stomach twisted. 'What do you mean? Did he have an accident? A fall?'

Cuts and bruises, broken bones. Injuries were temporary. Fixable.

'No,' Charlie said. 'I've been trying to show him how to build things, but he wouldn't listen. You have to be nice, you have to ask, you—'

'Where is he?' Olivia said.

Charlie jerked her head towards the house. 'He's asleep.'

Inside, Charlie's sleeping bag was opened out and flat. Leo's was zipped up, his unruly brown hair spilling over the top. Olivia edged closer.

'Leo? It's Olivia. Are you okay?'

No response.

She crouched down, carefully, by his side. 'Leo? Can you hear me?'

Still nothing. Olivia shook his shoulder and it crumbled under her hand, releasing a puff of foul-smelling air.

She coughed and whipped her head aside. 'Oh, Leo,' she said.

His body, shrivelled and desiccated, lay in the foetal position. His face was hollow, the skin stretched tight. In some places it had torn, revealing mottled bones underneath. A length of one of the grey weeds, torn and lifeless, lay underneath him.

Two nights ago, she'd been teaching him campfire songs. Now he looked like he'd been dead for months.

Olivia let her head drop. This wasn't supposed to happen. The kids were supposed to be all right.

The kids were supposed to live. She took a deep breath and it turned into a sob.

Charlie appeared behind her. 'Is Leo better now?'

'No, honey. No, I'm afraid he's not.'

Olivia held out her arms and Charlie walked into them. 'Are we going to be all right?' she said.

Olivia stroked her hair. She dug deep for confidence, for reassurance, and found only dust.

The kids were supposed to live.

'I don't know,' she said. 'I don't know, Charlie.'

The girl rested in her arms for a while longer, then pulled back. She wiped her eyes. 'I'll bury him,' she said, 'and we can say goodbye.'

'Charlie, I—'

'It's all right. I can dig. I know what to do. We used to have a cat, and it was called Oscar, and it got very old, and we dug a hole in the garden. And I helped, and my granny said I was brave, and that Oscar would be happy in the garden because it was pretty. The garden here isn't very pretty now, but I think Leo will still be happy, because we're here and he's not on his own. He didn't like being on his own.'

Olivia put a hand on her throat, tried to massage away the ache. 'Okay,' she said. 'Okay. We'll do that.'

At the back of the house, the patio had sunk into the earth. A wooden pub-style bench, tilted and half-submerged, stuck out from the brown, crisped lawn. Olivia cleared away a tangle of blackened

177

rose bushes and rotted fence panels, and Charlie scraped out a shallow trench.

'Ashes to ashes,' Olivia began, and could go no further.

Charlie stood with her head bowed, then raised her hand and waved. 'Bye,' she said.

Olivia closed her eyes. When she opened them, one of the spiny grey weeds was already snaking over the freshly turned earth. She reached for it, but Charlie grabbed her arm.

'No,' she said. 'Leave it.'

'All right,' Olivia said, and let Charlie take her back inside. The duvet she'd brought with her had more holes than material, but she spread it on the ground anyway and lowered herself awkwardly down. The baby kicked, a fluttering pain.

'Hello, Miranda,' Olivia said, and her voice cracked.

Charlie's face lightened. 'Is it the baby?' she said. 'Can I feel?'

Olivia took the girl's hand and laid it on her stomach. Miranda kicked again and Charlie gave a start. 'Hello, Miranda,' she said, and smiled. 'Will she be coming out soon?'

'I think so,' Olivia said.

'That's good,' Charlie said, then cocked her head. 'Isn't it? Olivia? Isn't it a good thing?'

Olivia closed her eyes. How was she supposed to answer that?

She'd had a plan, once. All arrangements carefully made and checked. She'd gone to classes, studied textbooks, bought everything she thought might be needed. The car always kept full of petrol, the lab's emergency number on speed dial. Robert had promised he would get there.

And then everything had gone to hell and she'd come up with a different kind of plan. To fight where others had given up. To beat the odds, because the kids were supposed to be all right. Because the kids were supposed to live.

Miranda kicked her again. Olivia put her head down and cried.

Charlie slipped a hand into hers. 'What are we going to do now?'

Olivia swallowed hard, scuffed a hand over her cheek. 'We're going to wait,' she said.

'Wait? Oh, you mean, for the baby?'

'Yes,' Olivia lied. 'For the baby.'

*** 

The sound of her name brought Olivia slowly, unhappily, out of sleep. 'No,' she said. 'Go away.'

Charlie shook her shoulder. 'Wake up. It's time to eat. You have to eat, it's for Miranda. You have to be eating for two, that's what my granny used to say.'

Olivia surfaced properly, rolling onto her elbow.

'Look, I found these,' Charlie said. She reached into a half-melted plastic bag and pulled out what looked like a flat, rough-textured mushroom. The cap was a dark grey colour, the underside black.

'They were growing outside. I think Leo made them. They're really nice.' She sank her teeth into it, the soft flesh tearing easily. 'Here,' she said. 'I got lots of them. These are for you.'

Olivia pushed it away. 'I don't want it. Go away, Charlie.'

'No. You have to eat.' She thrust it out again.

'I said I don't want it. I don't want anything.'

'You have to. It's for Miranda. She'll want it. Come on, Olivia.' She grabbed Olivia's hand and thrust one of the mushrooms into it. 'Eat.'

Olivia groaned. It was warm to the touch and slightly damp. She held it up to her nose, smelled dark earth. Not unpleasant. Her stomach rumbled.

Charlie smiled and nodded. 'It's good,' she said. 'Eat it.'

Olivia pushed her away again. 'Stop it, Charlie. Leave me alone.'

'No.' Charlie sat back on her heels, her face stubborn. 'We're going to have breakfast and then we're going to do chores. We have to get everything ready.'

'Chores?' Olivia laughed. 'Oh, Charlie. There are no chores, not any more. That's all over. Finished. Everything's finished.'

'No, it's not,' Charlie said. 'Come on, we have to make a new house. For Miranda.' She pulled at Olivia's sleeve.

'I can't. I just—I can't.'

'Yes, you can. It's not that hard. I can show you. Look.'

Charlie got up and grabbed one of the spiny weeds that climbed in and out of the shattered walls. She winced as the thorns dug into her palm and a drop of blood, thick and dark, slid down the weed's grey surface. It sank in, leaving no trace. Charlie lifted her hand, pulling the weed with her. She stepped back and kept going. The weed came too, coiling smoothly out of the broken foundations. At its base, it was thicker than Olivia's arm.

Charlie let it go, but it didn't drop. It kept moving, following her. She grasped another, held it up next to the first. They joined, flowing and blending together into a course, fibrous growth a foot wide, arching over Charlie's head. She pulled her hand down and it stayed in place.

She turned to Olivia and beamed. 'See?'

Olivia stared. 'How did you do that?'

Charlie shrugged. 'You just do. You have to let them bite you first and then they'll do what you want.' She hauled on another weed and joined it to the first two, making a half-dome. 'It's going to be an igloo,' she said. 'We could pretend we're explorers.'

Olivia huffed out a breath that turned into a surprised laugh. Slowly and painfully, her ears ringing, she got up.

The weed-structure looked firm. Solid. She looked at it from all angles, her eyes wide.

Charlie took up one of the smaller weeds, held it out. 'Now you try.'

Olivia hesitated, then put out a tentative hand. The weed wrapped itself around her palm, loosely at first, then tighter. The thorns broke the skin and sank into her flesh. Blood, rich and red, flowed down her arm. She gasped and instinctively pulled her injured hand close to her chest. The weed came with it.

181

'It's okay,' Charlie said. 'It only hurts for a little while.'

But the pain didn't stop. It burned, fierce and hot, through her muscles. The weed tightened its grip, the spines feeling as if they were clawing at the bone. She shrieked and tried to shake it off, but she couldn't dislodge it.

'Don't,' Charlie said. 'Don't do that.'

The weed plumped up and more of it came shooting out of the ground. It draped itself across her shoulders, the thorns like a rush of bee stings, then wrapped around her. Coiled lazily around her chest, her arms, her stomach. Dug in.

She beat at it, trying to yank it out, but it was stuck fast. Blood soaked through the thin, stretched material of her t-shirt, blooming into dozens of little flowers. She screamed again.

Charlie began to cry. 'You have to let it,' she said. 'You have to let it, Olivia.'

A lightning burst of pain blazed through Olivia's stomach, lighting up every nerve ending and arching her spine. Sudden, wet warmth told her what was happening. She gasped out Charlie's name. 'The baby's coming,' she said. 'The baby's coming now.'

'Don't fight it,' Charlie said. 'They won't hurt you if you don't fight.'

Pain forced Olivia to the ground. Blood continued to flow, but slower now. More sluggish. She watched it turn black, then closed her eyes and let the pain sweep her away.

\*\*\*

Olivia turned over the earth in the garden with a rake improvised from a broom handle and broken glass. Satisfied, she scattered a handful of seed pods for the things she still called mushrooms and poked them down into the warm, damp ground. A tiny shoot nuzzled her finger, nipped it gently.

A familiar cry broke the silence and Charlie came out of the igloo with Miranda in her arms. 'I think she's hungry.'

Olivia took the baby and handed the seed bag to Charlie. 'I'll feed her; you carry on with the planting.'

'Okay,' Charlie said, and bent over the furrowed earth.

Olivia sat down with her back against the weed walls of their home and guided the squalling baby to her breast. Miranda hushed immediately, little teeth sharp like thorns against Olivia's skin.

She suckled, pausing every now and then to coo happily. Olivia smiled and wiped away a drop of black milk from the baby's chin. She laid a kiss on the top of her head and lay back, inhaling the warm, earthy scent of her skin.

# Closer (Carrie Mills)

There are people better qualified for this, but there's no budget for a man like him. He will be in here for the rest of his life and I'm the best they have to offer. A shrink who gets an hour a week to fix a lifetime of trauma and a crumbling room with cheap artwork.

"Tell me about your mother."

"My mother? I don't want to talk about my mother, I told you that."

He sits across from me, rocking back and forth in his wheelchair; his one good hand absent-mindedly moving, the motion uneven.

This is our fourth session now, Ben talks freely, but he doesn't trust me. To him this is all a punishment he doesn't understand. She was younger than him and he went into eyes wide open.

"Did you talk about your mother with Karen?"

"Of course, we talked about everything; we didn't have any secrets. She listened."

"What did you tell her?"

"Everything."

"How do you think she felt about what you told her?"

"She was cross. Actually, it made her so angry that she cried a few times."

"What made her angry?"

"The physical stuff mostly. I showed her my scars and it made her sad. She said she could see the pain in them and she knew."

"She knew?"

"Knew what it was like. She had her own scars too. It's why she said we were so special."

He leans forward.

"When something like that happens to you, you can sense it in other people, and it makes you closer. No one else could understand that."

"You felt very close to her?"

"Not straight away. She said I had trust issues, took me a long time to tell her stuff. It took even longer to let her touch me. I did in the end though. She was patient, never pushed it. Like I said, she understood me."

"How did it feel, trusting her?"

"Well, it was good, wasn't it? To have someone who gets you; can see past everything and still love you just the same."

"Did she tell you that she loved you?"

"Lots. Every day. Said it was important to say it every day, so that I knew, so that I never doubted her. She loved me."

"Did you love her?"

"She took care of me when no one else gave a shit. She never judged me for crying, or hiding, or for being afraid."

He leans back.

"Did you love her?"

His hand goes back to the wheel.

"I loved her. I would have stayed with her too, but other people don't always understand, do they? They don't know what it's like to be us, to have never been loved, to know you won't ever find anyone who loves someone like you."

"How did you show her that you loved her?"

185

"She never made me have sex with her, if that's what you're asking. She said it would be unethical in her position as my therapist. She wanted me that way, I could tell, but she never pushed me."

"Did you want to have sex with her?"

"Yeah, I did. She was beautiful. She would hold me all the time and I really did then, but she didn't think it was a good idea. She said it would ruin something special. That we needed to be more than that. That we needed to be closer than even that."

"Closer how?"

"Closer in every way. Our love would make us live like a part of each other. We needed to be so together that you couldn't find the edges with your fingers."

"Is that what she said?"

"She said it, but we both knew it. Sometimes when we were holding each other, just like that, I would squeeze her so tight. I wanted to push her right inside myself, so we would always be together."

"Did you ever hurt her?"

He turns his wheelchair, so he's looking out of the window, and I can only see one side of his face.

"I never meant to. It made me sad when I hurt her, I wasn't trying to hurt her, I just didn't want to let her go. I didn't like it when she would go."

Where did she go?"

"Just to the shops and things. I don't like being on my own."

"What happens when you're on your own?"

He doesn't say anything for a while, motionless. Then he looks down at his hands, turns them over and goes back to looking out of the window. His voice is barely audible when he speaks.

"She used to lock me in a cupboard, my mother. As I got bigger it was harder to get me in there. After a while your body starts to hurt from being in the same position, when you can't move. I knew better than to make a fuss, but I would cry. Quietly as I could. I don't like being on my own in a locked place."

"Did she lock you in?"

"So I wouldn't follow her. We needed to be careful that no one saw me. I wasn't supposed to be there."

"Did you ever leave the house?"

"Not so much. I must have done, but I don't remember."

"Were you happy there?"

"Happiest I'm ever likely to be. I had Karen, and she loved me, and she didn't mind me exactly how I am."

"Exactly how you are?"

"I'm hard to live with. Needy. I need a lot of love she said, a lot of time and hard work. She said I was worth all of it though, and she would take care of me. Love me better than anyone had before."

"She loved you?"

He turns back towards me, grips the wheel tight so the blood drains from his fingers.

"I said that didn't I? We were in love in a way other people don't understand. We had to be careful, had to work hard, had to promise to be willing to let the other person have everything."

"Everything?"

"Talk honestly; be open and honest. Never lie and never leave. We were building something special."

"Tell me about mealtimes?"

Another pause, he weighs me up.

"I'm just here to listen."

"Don't suppose it matters now anyway. After we changed everything we could, after we had told each other everything, we still needed to get closer."

"Closer?"

"Closer. We needed to be a part of each other in every way, nothing held back. So, we started to share food. We shared one meal, ate it naked, holding each other, feeding each other."

"Was it only mealtimes?"

"No. Bath times, sleeping, crying. We did it all like we were one person. She was amazing, she made it so nothing else could get in. I was protected because she loved me, so nothing else could get in."

"But you sometimes hurt each other?"

"I didn't say that. I hurt her a couple of times, but she never hurt me. Never, the whole time, even when I lost it or was being weak. Even then."

He looks down at his hands again, flinching he goes back to staring out of the window. He's hiding his eyes from me.

"What happened?"

He sighs, "I wanted to have sex. I thought it was what was coming next, even though she told me we never would, I didn't believe her. She was nothing but good to me and honest and I let my own stupid fucking cock convince me otherwise. What kind of an arse hole am I?"

He shakes his head, amused.

"Did you have sex with her?"

"No, she didn't want to. And I didn't fucking rape her, Christ." The rocking starts up, slow, punctuated by running over a crease in the rug.

"I got angry though, shouted at her. Told her it was what I needed to feel closer to her. I slapped her when she tried to walk away; she hit her head when she fell down. I hit her when all she did was love me."

"How did you feel?"

"Do you get paid on a special rate to ask that question or something?"

"How did she react?"

"Just stood up, walked right up to me and held me even tighter. See, she knew me, she loved me and she forgave me even though I was weak and stupid."

"She wasn't angry or upset?"

"She said she was upset that I felt that way, that it must hurt me to feel angry with her. It did too, she was right. I loved her more than anything and I could have died right there I felt so bad."

"Were you still close after that?"

"It did change something she said, it showed we needed to do more. We weren't doing enough."

"More?"

"Mm," he nods.

He sets his gaze on me, but he's not really there.

"We were special, in a way other people can't ever be. We had a chance to be the closest two people can. Two souls coming together."

"Your souls?"

"Every human is born with a soul. Some are meant to be connected to each other, and if you can find those ones, then you can join them together, so that it's like being one person. That's the dream, isn't it? To never be on your own ever again. Our love would make us one, just like in those love songs we were listening to."

"What do you have to do to join two souls together?"

The question animates him, and he wheels himself closer, his hand alternating wheels so that he weaves toward me until he stops. Pulling himself forward on his seat; challenging me.

"She knew all the ways to help our souls come together so we could be happy. It's why we worked so hard, and we didn't let anyone distract us. We needed to live like we were already connected and find ways to be even closer physically. Our minds were already working together really well from what we'd done. We knew each other's thoughts and feelings just like they were the same thing as our own. Sharing our lives, eating, crying and talking, we had all that down. We just needed to keep pushing through."

"Tell me about the first time you tried to push through?"

He leans back again and looks over my shoulder while he talks.

"She went out, like she did, to get the food for us and stuff. She came back with dinner and a bag like doctors carry. She'd been talking to someone she said, found them online. They knew a way."

He's fidgeting again, rolling back and forth, watching the dominant wheel as it moves out of synch.

"It didn't hurt. She never hurt me. Just a small step each day she said. A small part of me becoming part of her.

She had a needle and injected the end of my finger. I felt it go numb, I could tap things with it and didn't feel anything. It sort of felt swollen but looked exactly the same.

The knife was one of those special ones they use in operations. Tiny cut, she said. I didn't feel anything, just let her hold my hand while she took a small slice from my finger and lay it on a plate. There wasn't too much blood, which is lucky because I don't like the sight of blood."

He looks at his hand, at where the finger was and smiles. He's not trying to hide his tears anymore.

"She asked me to feed her like I always did, so I took the flesh and placed it on her tongue. It was beautiful."

"Did she tell you what was going to happen?"

"She explained it. I was becoming part of her, and she would become part of me."

"Did she do that? Become a part of you as well?"

"I was first. Then she said that, when it was my turn to have part of her, I would be getting myself

191

back too, but better. It would make me whole again."

He looks down at where his legs were; where his hand was.

"Now I won't ever be whole."

What am I doing here?

# Bequeathed (Paul Edwards)

Way before the sickness, way before the decline and transformation, I visited forty-one Blackhart Hill – a nondescript council house opposite the flats where the Ragman lived.

It was a brittle, bright October morning. I drifted to the door and knocked twice on its frosted pane of glass. A curtain twitched so I knew somebody was home.

The door jolted open, an elderly man peering out at me. His back was hunched, his hair white, his fingers long and bent and twisted by arthritis. "Mr Benedict?" I asked and he nodded. "Got your message. I'm your local Police Community Support Officer."

He glanced over my shoulder at some indeterminable spot behind me, then ushered me inside, closing the door behind us.

The front room was small and cramped and smelled of cigarettes, damp and furniture polish. It was furnished with a couple of uncomfortable looking armchairs, a longcase clock, a coffee table and a stained, hard knotted rug.

He gestured for me to sit with a small wave of his hand. "Cup of tea?"

"No," I said, "thanks."

He eased himself into the chair opposite mine. "Thank you for coming. It's actually quite nice to have some company for a change." He looked up at the window. "Oh," he said, rising, beckoning me, "let me show you what the problem is."

I found my feet, watching him pull the curtain back to reveal the flats opposite. "There's something going on over there," he said. "Kids coming and going all hours of day and night. Not just kids sometimes. They knock on the window to number thirty-two, wanting to be let in."

He snatched the curtain shut again.

"I'll keep an eye on it," I said. "If you recognise anyone going in there, pass me their names. Also, any vehicles you see outside the address; try and get their indexes. I'll give you my mobile number and email address before I go."

There was a framed photograph standing on the windowsill, worn and faded, but I discerned a woman with long grey hair and a bright, pretty smile. "Your wife?" I asked, nodding at it.

"Aye," he said and sighed. "She died last year."

"Oh. Sorry to hear that."

"After she died, I didn't think I could cope with being alone." He knuckled his left eye. "They say time heals. Well, things haven't got any better for me, that's for sure."

Back at the station, I told Clare, my beat manager, about the flat.

"Have a look on Quickaddress and find out who lives in number thirty-two," she said, grabbing her hat and radio. "Got to dash – Shopwatch meeting in half an hour. Sounds like you got some good intel there, Keith."

She paused, picking a loose strand of hair away from her eyes. "I was on your patch the other day. Blackhart Hill, Crow Lane, Silver Street." She fastened her radio to the front of her body armour. "The residents there seem *defeated*. The gardens are a mess, there's junk heaped up in the streets. It feels like people are giving up, you know?"

I nodded. "But what can we do? I've been talking to the council and some local businesses about possibly funding a youth club or internet café, but no one's willing to put down the cash."

"Drugs are an easy escape." She snatched up a set of keys from off her desk. "Might be worth knocking on number thirty-two – see who's there, scope it out a bit."

"Think I will."

"Good luck," she said, and left.

Terri was watching TV when I got home. I kicked off my boots and entered the lounge. "What's this crap?" I asked, nodding at the unconvincing actress crying onscreen.

Terri didn't reply.

I walked into the kitchen, opened the fridge and grabbed myself a beer. "Remember they've got to last you all week," she shouted.

"Whatever," I mumbled back.

The credits were rolling when I returned and Terri was sat forward in her chair, her eyes red-rimmed and puffy. "What's up?"

She stared at her hands. "Tired, that's all."

We were quiet for a moment. I perched myself on the edge of the armchair, watching names scroll down the TV screen. "How's Joseph?"

"Asleep."

195

"Aren't you going to wake him? I mean, he won't sleep tonight if he…"

"What do you care?" she snapped, turning on me. "I'm the one who gets up, remember?"

I closed my eyes, concentrating on the sound of the traffic outside.

"How's work?" she asked at last.

I opened my eyes and glared at her. "I don't want to worry you with it. You've got enough to worry about, looking after Joseph all day." *You're always tired,* I thought with a stab of resentment, getting up, walking out of the room and leaving her to her soaps.

Joseph was sound asleep in the nursery, his tiny fists clenched tight, his eyelids twitching. I stroked his face, trying to feel something.

"Gorgeous, isn't he?" Terri whispered and I turned to see her in the doorway, leant against its unvarnished frame, her arms folded across her chest.

"Yes," I said and fixed a smile in place.

She walked to the cot and drew the blanket up over his shoulders. I stood there watching, guilt stealing over me. "It was something Clare said," I blurted as she straightened, her long hair shrouding her face.

"Sorry?"

"Clare. From work." I cringed at the slight tremor I heard in my voice. "We were talking about my beat. She said the people living on Blackhart Hill, Silver Street, Crow Lane… they all seem *defeated.* There's a resignation about them… people don't seem to care about anything anymore. Made me feel like shit, as if I'm not doing enough."

She touched my face. "Oh, Keith," she said, tilting her head to one side. "We've talked about this before. You're perfectly suited to that role because you *care*." Her hand dropped away and she smiled.

Later, while she was showering, I called Kate on my mobile. She answered almost immediately. "My sister's round in a minute. I'm busy. What...?"

"Can I see you tomorrow?" I interrupted, glancing nervously around at the door.

Kate's twenty-one and lives on her own in Silver Street. She had a problem with kids kicking footballs against her window and we got chatting and hit it off... in more ways than one.

"Don't know," she said. "I've got to take Mum to her hospital appointment."

"What time?" The shower stopped. I heard Terri pull back the shower curtain and step out of the bathtub.

"Three o'clock."

"I'm on an early. I could pop in during the morning."

A pause. Then, when she answered, I could almost picture the smile on her thin, painted lips. "You be in uniform?"

"Of course."

Terri opened the bathroom door.

"Gotta go," I said, killing the call. Then I smiled and got up and fetched myself another beer.

"I'm moving to Birmingham."

197

Kate's flat was poky and dimly-lit. On the sofa, my radio crackled; a road traffic collision involving a car and a push bike. It wasn't anywhere near the Blackhart estate, so I didn't have to worry about it.

Our clothes lay strewn around us on the floor. "You're not coming back?" I asked, sitting up on one elbow, my voice small and brittle sounding.

Kate flashed me a smile. "I'm making a go of things with Seb."

"Why?"

"Because I love him."

I laughed. "But you've been sleeping with me."

"And it's been good," she said, stroking the knuckles of my hand, "right? But we both knew it wouldn't be permanent."

I lay my head in her lap. "I'll miss you," I said, after a pause.

She stared at me and at last I met her eyes, trying, and failing, to understand what they were conveying.

Kate was silent as she watched me get dressed. The radio crackled – the controller directing a unit to an incident in Locksley. I wasn't even listening. "If you aren't happy you should leave her," Kate said, pulling on her bathrobe.

"Who says I'm not happy?"

"Oh, Keith."

"Good luck," I said, shrugging into my body armour and making for the door.

I walked up Silver Street, throwing one last look over my shoulder. She was staring out of her window, her expression one of discernible relief.

I kept on walking until I reached the top of Blackhart Hill. Broken fence panels shivered faintly in the wind. I made my way over to the flats, seeing Mr Benedict – pale, gaunt, unshaven – at his front window. I waved listlessly at him but he didn't wave back.

I turned to the flats and pushed at the door, discovering it unlocked. The communal hall stank strongly of piss. I closed the door behind me and turned to the flat on my left.

The door to thirty-two stood ajar, its handle hanging limp and broken above the letterbox. I peered in cautiously and saw two youths talking to somebody just out of my line of sight. One kid had short dark hair and a pimpled face, a leather coat draped over his shoulder. "I know you're not asleep," he hissed. "*Look* at me!" He stormed across the room, disappearing from sight.

The other youth – dressed in a combat jacket and black *Cradle of Filth* T-shirt – looked up and around, the colour draining from off his face. "Shit," he said, and the door was suddenly snatched open, the first youth reappearing before me. "Oh," he said. "Hi."

"What's going on?" I asked.

"Just leaving," the youth muttered, brushing past me, pushing out of the main door and exiting the flats. The other youth followed, glancing sheepishly at me as he left.

I turned my attention to the flat, to the open door and poked my head inside. "Hullo?"

The flat was unpainted, dirty and the stench of what might have been rotten fruit carried in the air.

There were hardly any furnishings – just an armchair pushed up against a wall in the corner. Slumped in it was an elderly man, his head lowered, his grubby hands clasped together in his lap. I couldn't see his face because his hair was in the way, but he was dressed in a filthy suit, shirt and waistcoat. Coarse, wheezing sounds bubbled in his throat.

For a moment I feared he was hurt; that I'd stumbled upon the scene of an assault, or worse.

"You okay?" I asked, standing over him. The male raised his head and I gasped. His face was covered in growths, pustules and sores. Black pus dribbled down the side of his misshapen nose from an ugly weal on his forehead. One of his eyes was swollen shut, his lips fat, split and moving wordlessly within a fiercely tangled beard.

He leaned forward, trying to touch me.

I instinctively stepped back.

He moaned as if he were trying to speak, to communicate, but I couldn't make out the words.

I gripped my radio, finger poised over the transmission button. My first thought was that he'd been beaten, that he was in need of emergency assistance. Then I realised those welts couldn't possibly have come from a beating... This was a medical affliction, signs of some horrible, debilitating disease. "Do you need help?" I said, crouching, feeling my face twist into a mask of disgust.

He shook his head, staring at the floor.

"Do you live here?" I asked, as loud and as clear as I could.

He nodded.

"Who were those kids?"

No reply.

"You should keep your door closed," I said, straightening, standing over him again. "Get the lock fixed."

I lingered there for just a moment longer, wondering if I should do anything more. "You sure you're all right?"

"Leeth *melone,*" he rasped, suddenly.

My shoulders sagged and I nodded at him, turned and left.

Terri was busy cooking Bolognese when I got in. She was wearing a short black dress with a ribbed low-cut top. "How was your day?" she asked as I stepped into the kitchen.

"Not bad." I peeled off my coat. "Where's Joseph?"

"Mum's." Her smile was tentative, barely a flicker. "Thought we could do with a night in on our own. Some quality *us* time, eh?" She gestured to the lounge with a nod of her head. "Sit down, dinner's almost ready. I'll bring it in in a sec."

We ate in front of the TV. Nothing much was on and I kept tuning into the sound of the rain scratching against the window. Once we'd eaten, I put our plates on the coffee table and turned to her.

A bittersweet smile spread across her face. "Sorry," she said.

"What for?"

"Yesterday. I was in a right old mood."

"It's all right."

"No. No it's not all right."

My gaze drifted back to the TV.

"I've had a really nice day," she said, stretching her legs out. "I've had my nails done and I bought myself a brand-new blouse from M&S. Caught up with Sara, too." Sara was Terri's sister.

She moved in close, smiling, but I pulled away before she could kiss me. "Sorry," I spluttered, "I'm tired. It's been a long day."

She sat back, stung. "Oh," she said, crossing her arms across her chest and sighing. "We never want it at the same time, do we. Maybe..." She tailed off.

She laid her head against me, then wrapped her arm around my waist. Moments later she was asleep.

I wanted to tell her everything then. Wanted to wake her up and make things right. Instead, I placed a hand over my face and sobbed quietly, ever-so-softly through my fingers.

Terri never stirred, never heard a thing.

The morning was cold and dark, rags of cloud drifting across the leaden sky. The rain held off until I reached Blackhart Hill, where Mr Benedict was tending to his garden. He'd cut back the grass, weeds and nettles and hung up a flower basket in his front porch. "Someone's been busy," I said, smiling over his hedge.

He looked up, a pair of secateurs in his hands. "Been meaning to do this for ages. Didn't have it in me before."

"You're looking well."

"Aye. Can't complain."

I nodded at the flats opposite. "Any more activity?"

His cheeks reddened and he pinched his nose. "Pretty sure there's nothing going on. Probably was reading too much into it."

Mr Benedict began snipping at his rose bush. "They're local residents," he said. "Good Samaritans, making sure he's okay."

"You've seen him?"

"Aye," he said, and I fancied for a moment he was vaguely irritated by me. "Visited him yesterday as a matter of fact." He rubbed the back of his hand in his cardigan. "Went round with the neighbours. As I said, it's perfectly innocuous." He shrugged. "Sorry I wasted your time."

Just as he finished speaking, four lads in hoodies stepped out of the flats. I looked up, listening in on their conversation.

"He's fucked," said one.

"What do we care?" said another. "As long as he sorts us out."

"What if he...?" began a third, then they noticed me, their eyes narrowing, their elbows nudging one another. Then they turned and walked off at speed, heading down Blackhart Hill. The first drop of rain struck my cheek as I spun, Mr Benedict, secateurs still in hand, watching me run.

I jogged past the vandalised telephone kiosk on the corner of Crow Lane, the Residents Centre, chip shop and the convenience store. Finally I reached Silver Street, seeing the youths duck beneath the old railway bridge. I quickened my pace, but by the time I reached the bridge they were nowhere to be seen. They must have scrambled up the embankment onto the tracks, I thought and turned back the way I had come. Then a figure emerged from the bushes beside the bridge and I recognised him instantly as the kid in the combat jacket and *Cradle of Filth* t-shirt from yesterday.

He stared at me, the wind driving his hair into his dead white face.

"Where are the others?" I asked.

"Gone home." He pulled in a breath. "I thought, perhaps, if I talked to you…"

"What's going on with that guy in the flat?"

His whole face was twitching, as though the flesh were trying to tear itself free of the skull. "D-don't take him away. What he can do…well, it's a miracle." The boy rubbed his nose, glancing nervously about us at the rain-lashed street. "People call him the Ragman. We *need* him – this *neighbourhood* needs him." He stepped away from me. "I-I shouldn't have… The others warned me…"

"Wait," I said, but he was off, running flat out, darting up Silver Street toward Blackhart Hill. I let him go, knowing I would never catch him.

I was still thinking about the incident later on that night, lying in bed next to Terri. I couldn't for the life of me sleep; too much was going on in my brain to switch off. I gave eventually and carefully climbed out of bed. A part of me wanted to wake Terri and tell her *everything,* but I now sensed there was an easier way of shedding my guilt. I wanted to cast off my disappointment over Kate going, too.

Despite the hour I left home and wandered the streets, ending up in the middle of the Blackhart estate. I knew I wouldn't be able to resist coming here; it was the ideal time for me to see him. Broken windows emitted drunken voices and the strong reek of cannabis. Dog shit made a minefield of the pavement.

I reached the flats at last, pushing through the unlocked main door. The communal hall was dark and still smelt of urine. I closed the door behind me, then turned to the flat on my left. The broken door widened as I shoved against it, stale, dust-choked darkness enveloping me.

I immediately discerned a familiar shape in the corner, seated in his armchair, and I walked over, crouching, my nose wrinkling in disgust. "I understand you can help," I said, trying not to breathe in that sickening smell of decay.

His head jerked to one side and a guttural moan escaped him. A cloud of flies shifted across his face. Then he reached out a hand and I nodded, smiled, and felt his fingers grip my shoulder. His good eye opened, glittering wetly in the dark. "Puh-puh-*puhleease*, g-g-god."

"Can you help me?" I asked, trying hard not to sound desperate. Then his eye began to cloud, to glaze over, his voice dropping to a whisper. *"At lassssst."* He released his grip.

Something was wrong.

I got to my feet, my head flashing with strange lights, shapes and colours. I felt weirdly nauseous and afraid. I reached out, grabbing his waistcoat and shaking him hard.

No response.

"Fuck," I whispered.

I straightened, glancing round at the door.

Phone someone. Get help.

Instead, I ran out the door and fled into night's uncaring arms.

Terri said, "Don't worry about it."

It was two weeks later. She was leant against the bathroom door as I was staring into the mirror at the sores that had appeared on my forehead, nose and neck. I touched them with trembling fingers before dropping my hand to my side and grimacing. One of them had split, oozing black pus.

She drifted toward me. Outside, rain hissed against the mottled windowpane and I thought I could hear thunder. She was naked, her hair hanging in her face. "Oh, that was *good*," she smiled, chewing her lip, her eyes shining behind her hair. "Can we do it again later?"

She reached out, stroking my arm. "You won't want me soon," I said, my gaze still glued to my image.

"Don't say that! *Course* I'll want you."

From the next room, Joseph began to cry.

"Uh-oh," she said.

"I'll go."

I rocked Joseph back off to sleep in my arms. I stared out the window, seeing only a dismal grey wall of rain. Once Joseph had settled, I lowered him into the cot and tugged his blanket over him. I touched his face with blistered fingers, then returned to our bedroom and Terri.

I got into bed. "Is he all right?" she asked.

"Fine."

"Hold me," she said, and I rolled over and held her.

Later, in the middle of the night, I woke with a violent start.

"What's wrong?" Terri asked, sitting up, throwing back our duvet and reaching for me.

"I can't see," I shrieked, clasping a hand over my eye. "I can't *see!*"

I ran into the bathroom, trying to squint and see my disfigured reflection in the mirror above the sink.

The skin around the left eye was puckered and swollen, the eyelid seemingly unable to lift. My skin was a shrivelled mess of fresh pustules, blisters and sores.

Terri flung her arms around me and told me everything was going to be all right, but I knew it wouldn't. Not now.

Not ever.


It's Friday night and I'm upstairs all alone in the bedroom. The curtains are drawn, the light switched off. I'm sitting on the edge of the bed, absently listening to the noises in the street. I've hung a white sheet over the mirror so I don't have to look at myself. I've been off work for three weeks and resigned myself to the fact that I won't be going back.

I feel bone weary tired and can barely eat or speak. I just sit and stare at the wall, or at the faded floral pattern on the curtains, or at the strange growths on the backs of my hands. The stench of rotten fruit seems to perpetually cling to me.

I hear the front door open, Terri and her sister Sara talking in hushed tones down in the hall. Sara lost her job last week and her husband's been diagnosed with prostate cancer. Terri told me she's in a bad place, which almost made me want to laugh out loud.

I can hear them mounting the stairs, Sara whispering something, Terri replying that it's going to be all right, that I can help, that I can siphon the pain and make everything better…

The bedroom door creaks open, Sara letting out a small, involuntary cry. I try to form a smile, but my mouth hurts and my lips split and weep a little.

Terri comes sweeping over, running her hand through my hair, kissing me and saying, "Oh, my love, my love."

With one watery eye I gaze at Sara, who looks upon me in horror. She turns to Terri and asks, "What do I do?"

Terri grins. "Go to him."

"Keith?" Sara whispers and I try to smile again, to speak, but the noise which leaves me is low, guttural and wrong. I hold out my arms in an automated fashion. Sara collapses into them, gasping, tears running down the length of her face and as I pull her in tight, I hope and pray to god to die.

# Meet the authors

**Olivia Arieti** lives in Torre del Lago Puccini, Italy, with her family. She writes drama, poetry and fiction. Her stories have appeared in several magazines and anthologies including, *Enchanted Conversations, Enchanted Tales Literary Magazine, Fantasia Divinity Magazine, Forgotten Tomb Press, Horrified Press, Infective Ink, Pandemonium Press, Sirens Call Publications, Blood Song Books, Black Hare Press, Pussy Magic Magazine, Stormy Island Publishing, Breaking Rules Publishing, Scarlet Leaf Review, Iron Faerie Publishing, Dark Dossier Magazine, Paramour Ink Press, Raven and Drake Publishing.*

**Gary Budgen** lives and works in London. His previous work has appeared in various magazines including Interzone, BFS Horizons, Morpheus Tales, Sein und Werden and the BFS Award short-listed anthology Humanagerie from Eibonvale. His work has been in many other anthologies from publishers including Thirteen O'Clock Press, Boo Books and Horrified Press. A collection of stories, Chrysalis, is published by Horrified Press and the chapbook Fragments of Onyx by Salo Press. A full publishing history can be found at garybudgen.wordpress.com.

**Dorothy Davies** is an editor, writer and medium. Somehow all these things come together in her seemingly crowded leisure and work life. She retired from editing for a while to run a second hand shop, the best one on the Isle of Wight, but the thrill of finding and publishing outstanding stories became too much so she started again with the Gravestone Press imprint. She still runs the shop...Her book, The Skullface Chronicles, the story of a zombie taking revenge on his dysfunctional family, is available through fiction4all.com. She has a store of short stories, some of which are finding their way into the anthologies, having not seen daylight for many a long year. She also channels books from spirit authors, notable figures from our history. These can be found on the Fiction4all site under Zadkiel Publishing.

**Paul Edwards** is a life-long horror fan and writes his own twisted tales in any spare time that he can grab. He has seen three collections of stories published – *Now That I've Lost You* (Screaming Dreams), *Black Mirrors* (Rainfall Books) and *Night Voices* (Demain Publishing), the latter being a joint-collection with author Frank Duffy. Paul is also a fan of role-playing games, rock music and rough Somerset cider.

**Jason R. Frei** lives in Eastern Pennsylvania where he works as a therapist with children and adolescents. He writes speculative fiction culled from the experiences of his life and those he works with and blends science fiction, fantasy and horror into new creations. His flash story "The Garden" will be featured in the horror anthology *99 Tiny*

*Terrors* by Pulse Publishing and his short story "Some of the Parts" will be featured in the horror anthology *Toilet Zone 3: The Royal Flush* by Hellbound Books Publishing. Visit him online: https://facebook.com/odinstones.

**Rickey Rivers Jr.** was born and raised in Alabama. He is a Best of the Net nominated writer and cancer survivor. His work has appeared in the JJ Outre Review, Stellium Literary Magazine, Fabula Argentea (among other publications).

**Rie Sheridan Rose** multitasks. A lot. Her short stories appear in numerous anthologies, including Killing It Softly Vol. 1 & 2, Hides the Dark Tower, Dark Divinations and On Fire. She has authored twelve novels, six poetry chapbooks and lyrics for dozens of songs. She is also editor-in-chief for Mocha Memoirs Press and editor for the Thirteen O' Clock imprint of Horrified Press. She tweets as @RieSheridanRose.

**Liam A. Spinage** is a former philosophy student, former archaeology educator and former police clerk who spends most of his spare time on the beach gazing up at the sky and across the sea while his imagination runs riot.

**SJ Townend** hopes that her stories take the reader on a journey to often a dark place and only sometimes back again. SJ won the Secret Attic short story contest (Spring 2020), has had fiction published with Sledgehammer Lit Mag, Hash

Journal, Ghost Orchid Press, Bandit Fiction, Black Hare Press, Black Petals Horror Magazine, Ellipsis Zine, Gravely Unusual, Gravestone Press, Holy Flea, Horla Horror and was long listed for the Women on Writing non-fiction contest in 2020. She has also written and self-published two dark mystery novels, both of which are available to purchase elsewhere: (Tabitha Fox Never Knocks, Twenty-Seven and the Unkindness of Crows). Follow her on Twitter: @SJTownend